Dance like a Poor Man

SAMUEL HOFER

HOFER PUBLISHERS

Canadian Cataloguing in Publication Data

Hofer, Samuel 1962-
Dance like a Poor Man
ISBN 0-9693056-6-4

1. Hutterian Brethren - Saskatchewan - Fiction.
I. Title.

PS8565.0326D3 1995 C813'.54 C95-920097-5
PR9199.3.H632D3 1995

Book design by Samuel Hofer
Cover illustrations: name withheld

This book was printed in Canada by
Prairie Graphics, Saskatoon, Sask., for Hofer Publishers.

Published by:
Hofer Publishers
P.0. Box 42035 - 1881 Portage Ave.
Winnipeg, Manitoba
R3J 3X7

The Hutterite community of Flat Willow in this novel is in no way related to the actual Hutterite community in Montana, USA, with the same name. This story is fictitious, as are the Hutterite communities and characters. Any resemblance to persons living or dead is purely coincidental.

For Erin, Jessica and Elliot:

I said I'd write you a children's book. If this is a children's book, it's the kind that bites.

Baraka Bashad

Chapter One

On lotday Sunday the sun climbed over the heavens hidden behind high, feathery clouds, and I stood outside our unit for a while in the afternoon, playing tricks on my eyes. I stared and squeezed, watching the blood hues rush together and become ghosts of the sun inside my head. Each time I let the light flood back in, I saw I was still at Rockyview Colony, and the blue Canadian Rockies rising up out of the foothills winked back at me. I listened for the wind. On lotdays, my father had said, the wind blew where it wished, and you heard the sound, but you didn't know where it would blow you till the preachers made the draw. I heard a calf bawling over at the corral, but that was all. There was just a wisp of a breeze on lotday, and you couldn't hear that.

I walked back into the foyer of our unit.

"And remember, Zack, what we talked," my mother was saying as she brushed something off my father's beard, and fussed a little with the collar of his white shirt to make sure it wasn't crooked.

"Now yes, Mother," he said. "But you know, not all people can be pleased with the outcome." He yanked on his black Sunday jacket, and his big strong hands worked on the buttons.

Then Judy asked what they would do in the big school.

"We will put about the same number of souls with each of the two preachers," he said, picking up his black hat off

Judy's palms, "and divide everything the community owns down the middle. Then the preachers will pull out the lot."

"But why, Father?"

My father took a deep breath and patted Judy's cheek. "Because, lieba, our community has gotten too big already, so we had to build up a new one."

Judy bit her lip and frowned. She seemed puzzled.

"What about Olvetter?" I said. "Will he be with our family?"

My father didn't answer *my* question. I figured he hadn't heard me, or was weary from the questions.

Long before lotday, he had told me how it worked. "It's completely easy," he had said. "On lotday you just throw your cowboy dreams out of your head and into the wind."

"Olvetter wants to stay," I had said.

"Your olvetter is an old man, you are a twelve-year-old kid." My father's nature was as calm as his grainfields when the wind was down.

I thought lotday was a noose flying over my head that could yank me completely out of Rockyview Colony to a flatland with no cows and no horse — just grainfields, and blizzards so dangerous that people froze to death. Well, it had happened. When the men built up Flat Willow, that's when it happened. They'd told all kinds of news about the new colony back there in Saskatchewan every time they came home for a weekend, and most people at the old colony were anxious to see the new-style houses and expensive barns the men were building. But whenever talk came up about the neighbour who had walked out in a storm and was found frozen dead the next day, the adults got uneasy and short on words, so you had to sharpen your ears and listen through walls and doors if you wanted to find anything out. Everybody knew the Kleinser boys had stolen a gun from one of the neighbours, but those buggers lied it away. Some of the Kleinsers at our colony were raw eggs. Especially the pigman. He was plain evil.

People who feuded against the Kleinsers said the man's death and the theft of the gun were connected, but my father said that ideas like that came from some loosewit's careless talk.

But my older sisters, now, they were something else. They weren't crazy like my brother Jake, but they could get pretty lappisch. When I said a few times that I might saddle up Madeline and hide out in the Rocky Mountains on lotday and refuse to move away from Rockyview, they joked and said, "Why, Peter, are you fearing that poor man's ghost will be there to haunt you?" Boy, that got my mother upset. She didn't stand for that talk, and you couldn't blame her. My grandmother's death was too fresh. "Let the dead rest," she said. "And it's a sin to speak that way about a poor man." I was just glad my sisters weren't teasing me about girls for a change.

Now, with my father out the door, my mother and my sisters watched after him through the corner window. There was no Sunday School that afternoon because of lotday, and with all the electricity in the air, I had no desire to take my nap, so I reached for my katus on the hat rack.

"Where are you going?" Anna's big eyes were on me.

"Hufer Miechel's house," I said.

"I know why you're going there," she sang out, twiddling wisps of her hair that always seemed to come loose from under her bonnet. Anna was nine years old, and when she wasn't babysitting for the Kleinser clan or playing tic-tac-toe and hopscotch with Rachel Wurz and her sisters, she hung around the Hufer family's unit like I did in my spare time. I showed her my fist and slipped out the door.

Outside, the men's backs were turned. They marched along the boardwalks that spanned the lawns like rulers, connecting the mouse-gray unithouses to the central huddle of other old shingle-covered outbuildings there. The big school sat at the far end of the yard, past the kuchel, and just past the little school. Some men had already stepped onto the boardwalks that ran up the middle of the yard. The two preachers strode in front.

Behind them walked the hauswirt, a small tschabadan, the suitcase that held his business papers, in hand.

When I walked into Hufer Miechel's unit, my aunt Katrina, looking tired, stepped from behind a wall of cardboard boxes piled to the ceiling.

"Is your mother finished packing?" she asked.

"Yes," I said. My mother had started early, as soon as the elders announced that the new colony was finished and lotday was only a week off.

Katrina-Pasel pointed to a box standing in the middle of the foyer on the hardwood floor. "Help me here, Wolner Peter," she said. "Hold your finger on the twine here while I make a knot."

I heard footsteps in the adjacent room, and Miechel's sister Maria appeared at the door. Her willowy arms were wrapped around a sleeping baby resting against her shoulder. She smiled and blinked her eyes really fast about six times, and I gave her my special smile too. Her apron usually hung crooked and she had braces on her teeth, but I always had a smile for her.

"Miechel will come back in a minute," she whispered. "Mother sent him for a pail of water from the washhouse."

I just kept smiling and feeling darn good. I didn't mind waiting, and I didn't mind that Miechel wasn't there. We were the cowboys of Rockyview Colony, but my head sometimes took vacations away from the cows.

* * * *

The old cowbarn stood at the bottom of the long hill that gave us exactly 335 feet of snow to coast down with our wooden sleds in the winter. Behind that hill, which we called the Big Hill, the foothills rolled away to the Rocky Mountains. The barn held eighty-five dairy cows. They nudged each other back and forth, chewing hay and drinking water, then rested in their stalls, making milk. "That's their job," my uncle Dan, the cowman, had said. Out behind, in the corrals, five hundred feeder cattle feasted on barley and alfalfa, guzzled water, and made piles of manure. You could see them get fatter and meatier as the weeks went by. "That's their life," Dan-Vetter said.

My grandfather had talked about the olden days, when Rockyview had very little money. During the Dirty Thirties they sometimes didn't wake the babies up till noon because there was nothing to feed them for breakfast. But one thing God blessed them with was plenty of fieldstones when they broke the land up. They hauled the good ones with strong horses and stoneboats and built up the barn. The shakes too on the dual-pitched roof, weathered silvery as an old rock, were the very ones that Olvetter and his already dead brothers had nailed up there. And in the year I was born, the men added on the milking parlour. Boy, I was loaded with pride about that. The barn connected me with the olden days. It was my barn. Actually, it belonged to all of the 135 souls at Rockyview, but I was one of the cowboys.

Hufer Miechel and I rolled alfalfa bales off the hay wagon. Below, my brother Jake set them onto the chain conveyer. Jake helped us do chores and milk the cows when Dan-Vetter was away.

Squeaking and rattling, the conveyor carried the bales through the doorway and to the feeding rack in the barn. The sweet and yeasty smell of alfalfa mingled with the dairy odour wafting through the barn door. To help the pasture along in mid-summer, we fed the cows in the barn at afternoon chores. Some were already swaying home, their udders swollen with milk.

"Will Flat Willow ever get a quoter?" Miechel asked.

"It's called a quota!" I said. The dairy board allowed only a certain number of dairy cows on the market, just enough to supply the milk it could use. It could take many years before the new colony got one.

"Are you worried?" Miechel asked.

"Hell yes," I said.

Jake tossed up a dried cowpie. "Stop yakkin', you two, and keep those bales coming or I'll fire you," he called out.

I laughed. Jake couldn't fire us. He acted like a tough worldman, that's how he was. Jake was nineteen years old. He made forbidden money with coyotes every winter. With the pelt money he had bought an extra-wide-brimmed hat and a pair of cowboy boots from the store in Lethbridge. His boots were too showy for church, even. When he clomped up and down the boardwalks, you could hear him from two hundred feet away. Jake was handsome, my older sisters said, although he was often stubbly and didn't shave till the preachers had to remind him that people who weren't baptised and married yet weren't allowed to wear beards. They became especially stern when he grew a moustache. Moustaches were completely forbidden because they made you look too much like a soldier.

"Drink time," Jake said as he flicked off the switch on the conveyer. He jiggled his black pants to shake clinging hay off, and stepped over to the bale by the wall where a half-pack of beer waited. Hufer Miechel and I made big eyes.

"What the devil are you staring for?" Jake smirked as he twisted the cap off a bottle. The bottle hissed.

"You know what Mother says."

"Oh yeah, I forgot, my brother is the preacher." Jake lifted the bottle to his mouth and his Adam's apple bobbed as he guzzled the beer down, grunting with satisfaction. When he came up for air, the bottle was already half empty. "She doesn't need to know about these, buster," he said.

In the milking parlour, Jake filled the stainless steel sink with warm water and I poured in a few ounces of chlorine disinfectant from a plastic jug. Jake made sure the suction cups on the rack were tight. Then he unscrewed the pipe that carried the milk to the stainless steel tank, and swung it over the sink.

"Okay boys, bring 'em in." My brother flicked the switch up and the pump whined into action. In seconds, the water was sloshing in the glass pipes overhead.

The cows were pushing against the holding pen gate. I swung it open. "Hi Betsy — hi Suzy — hi Daisy. " I gave each cow a pat on the neck as they filed into the pen. Cows were my favourite animals. Especially the dairy cows. They were gentle and smooth, and you could tell by the way they blinked their eyes at you and slowly chewed their cuds that they were at peace.

A long time before, Jake had loved the cows too. I knew that because he had named many of them when *he* was the cowboy. But he wasn't serious any more. "You're too serious," he always told me. I even drew westerns about a cowboy named The Cowboy Kid, that's how darn serious I was about being the cowboy. It was Jake who'd given me *Billy the Kid* and *The Rawhide Kid* comic books to read when I was ten, which got me started on my own westerns. But Jake didn't read much now. And he didn't really care about the cows, either. If you'd have ever come to Rockyview Colony and met Jake, I'll bet he wouldn't even have mentioned the cows, even though the cows were most important to Rockyview. He'd probably have invited you over to the pigbarns instead for a drink with Kleinser Chuck, the pigman. He had stuck with the Kleinsers ever since my oldest sister Dorothea married into their clan. If you'd have asked *him* about that gun that disappeared back in Saskatchewan, he'd have told you flat out to mind your own cottonpicken' business, to keep your nose out of our colony's affairs.

Inside the holding pen, the cows waited patiently for their turn to be let into the parlour, six at a time. We wiped the dirt and dust from their teats, then slipped on the milkers. The pump went *tsketuk*, *tsketuk*, *tsketuk*, *tsketuk*; the sound was like slaps of water inside a great cave. The sweet smell of raw milk and cows hung in the parlour, and the milk hurried along the pipes to the cooling tank.

"Go on out 'n feed the calves," Jake said, as he pulled another bottle of beer from his case. "I can handle 'em by myself for a while."

Madeline, the horse, was among the calves. She trotted toward us, eager to nuzzle our hands. I set the pail of barley chop down and reached up to pull her sweaty neck against my shoulder. "Boy oh boy," I said. "If I move I think I'll die, Madeline."

Madeline pulled up quickly and her halter flapped noisily. "No way, boy, you aren't moving," she seemed to say.

In the shine of her big, dark eyes I saw the Rockies and the blue sky. As Dan-Vetter's summer helpers for two years, Hufer Miechel and I had had the privilege of riding Madeline. The elders elected one manager to every job in the community, and all the livestock managers then chose one or two helpers. When we rode Madeline in the foothills, I felt as if I was just my soul, free and alone like the wind. Hufer Miechel and I made it our secret job to protect the range cows from dangerous outlaws and wild beasts.

"Remember that time we rode too near the mountains and saw the lynx?" Miechel asked. "You told Madeline if she got us home safely, you would brush her every day for three weeks."

I laughed. "And I kept my promise, didn't I?"

* * * *

The brethren were coming from the big school. My mother said the cooks in the kuchel wouldn't need to delay supper after all. Women and children were waiting on the boardwalks. I lined up too. Suddenly, the high-pitched whine of the milking pump at the cowbarn went dead. My uncle Dan's woman, who did the cleaning up, had just shut it off. My father, Dan-Vetter, Josh-Vetter, and Olvetter were coming toward us. Behind them walked Hufer Miechel's father. Anna and Judy blocked the men's path.

"Father, are we moving? Are we?" They bounced and flapped their arms.

Anna had told me most of the school girls at Rockyview

had already polished their low-style shoes, starched their polka-dot kerchiefs and packed apple cases full with their stuff. And now, Anna and Judy were showing off their new calico skirts and bodices that my older sisters had made for wearing at Flat Willow Colony. That's how sure they were we'd move.

"We'll be on Kleinser Isaac's side." My father acted as if it was just a small thing.

"But Father, tell us where *our* preacher will be."

He grinned. "Well, let's see — "

"Zack, stop teasing the children." My mother was also waiting on the steps. Her whole body bounced to her laugh.

"We won't be living in Alberta any more," he said, and my sisters hopped with glee on the boardwalks. They rushed into the house to tell the older sisters, whose faces were in the windows. Every house at Rockyview had faces in the windows.

"What about Hufer Miechel's family?" I asked.

"Not everybody can move," my father said.

Hufer Miechel's father strode in the same determined way he always did, but his face told a different story. Miechel and Maria and all the little Hufer children ran to greet him at their unit. He put his arms around Miechel and Maria.

"We're staying," he said. "And we'll be here for at least another fifteen years now. Let's go help your mother unpack those boxes."

In the foyer of our unit, my sisters chattered like geese over fresh grass. My older sister had seen the new colony already, when they'd gone to Saskatchewan to paint the communal dining hall and the kuchel. They'd raved plenty about Flat Willow. I figured their heads had been up in the clouds ever since. But I stood at the window, silent, stubborn. I remembered a drawing of God's finger pointing down from heaven, chasing Adam and Eve from the Garden of Eden. I flashed away quickly. I didn't want to think about God speaking to me.

Anna walked up behind me and carelessly placed her hand on my shoulder. "Hi Gooseboy," she said.

Chapter Two

Another light rose out of the dark. As the truck clanged over the cattle crossing, I heard the motor whine down. The driver shifted into low gear, and slowly the headlights drew nearer. He swung left at the turnoff near the rootcellar and the chickenbarns, and drove to the Kleinser clan's unithouse. The tires made a grinding sound on the gravel road.

I sat on the house steps with my grandfather and Anna.

"Rush, rush, rush," the old man grumped. "As if people were afraid there'd be work left over at the end of the world."

Rockyview was usually still at night — and dark, with only three yardlights on poles. But on lotday, every family's porchlight was burning. And trucks from other colonies arrived regularly, noisily backing up to people's doors. Rockyview was like a town out in the world, filled with lights and noise and exhaust fumes.

I saw my mother through the open window behind me, giving orders. She wore a pencil against her plump cheek, between her hair and kerchief, and she kept checking her spiral notepad. Umpteen boxes of clothes and fabrics, many jars of old Christmas sweets and canned fruits, a few pots and pans, and our soap supply were stacked in the living-room. She reminded my older sisters Lena and Lisbeth about five times to make absolutely sure that the men padded the varnished beds, chairs and drawer-cabinets with cardboard when they lifted them onto the truck-box. My father and Jake had removed the attic staircase and the landing, and were lowering our painted storage chests down the stairwell with yellow ropes. I could tell Jake was still feeling his drinks. He had a lot of oomph, as if he were preparing to slaughter a steer. But he wasn't too steady. My mother pressed her lips tight when she looked at him, as if she were trying to hold something inside. My father was quiet until Jake let the rope slip too fast. "For heaven's sake, Jake," he said. "Don't you know when to quit?"

The house door opened and my sister Sara came out. She stood behind me and reached down to gneip my shoulders a little. Boy, it felt good. She was a good gneiper because her hands were strong as hydraulics. Whenever my mother's shoulders ached, she'd ask Sara to rub away the pain with those thick fingers of hers. She was fifteen years old already. And she wore big glasses. The boys from the Kleinser clan sometimes teased her and called her a muttela because she was thickset, and looked like a little mother already.

"But Olvetter, that's how the moving goes these days," she said when the old man complained about the rush again. "We have to keep up with everybody else."

"Will it end soon, Olvetter?" Anna asked.

"The moving?"

"No, the world. Will it end soon?"

"Yes, child — soon."

"Ankela would have wanted to move," Sara said.

Anger rose in Olvetter's voice. "Who told you such a thing? Fifty-five years we lived here. Now we have to move."

"She died, Olvetter." Sara was direct.

"You be quiet, girl!" Olvetter said, shaking his finger at her. "You have respect now."

He looked up and I followed the old man's gaze to the starry sky. People sometimes gossiped about him, and said he'd become aloof after our grandmother died. He stood every day in silence for a while at the dairybarn window. Someone from the Kleinser clan had started a rumour that Olvetter was praying for

God and Jesus to come down and end the world so he could be with Ankela. I figured that one was probably true. He talked about the end of the world a lot.

I felt a soft wind brush my face. With the change in the air came a minty smell of grass and dirt of a marsh or something. I thought about the geese and the wheat fields in Saskatchewan. The millela on top of my family's outhouse rattled into action. I had carved the little propellor from a cedar shingle that the wind blew off the cowbarn.

Another truck arrived. This one came toward our unit.

"Our movers are here!" Sara scurried inside to tell the others. My mother had promised her brother Petch and his two sons, Christoph and David, the opportunity to be our movers. They had come from Moon Ranch Colony down close to Montana. Lena and Lisbeth pressed into the window, waving as if they were in a waving match.

"Hello, hello," Petch said as he stepped from the tandem GMC truck. "Do we call you Flat Willow people already?"

In the house, the adults all gave each other the hand. There were many "How goes it?" and "Oh, we can't complain" greetings. Lena and Lisbeth pushed together two tables in the foyer and laid out snacks. Sara placed a kettle on the little electric cooker sitting on a chair and the smell of coffee filled the house. We all squeezed around the table. My father asked us to take our hats off then so he could pray. My brother left his hat on, and my mother got really serious and told him flat out that he was no heathen. "Christians take their hats off at the table," she said. Some odd looks went around, and Jake took off his hat.

The adults each drank a glass of beer, and we all lunched on crackers, canned peaches, and chocolate bars. My sisters tried hanging the nickname "Petch" on me. But my mother didn't go for that. "He is too young for a nickname," she said.

"His nickname is Cowboy," Jake said, and I smiled. I liked it when people called me Cowboy.

"Cowboy, hmm?" Petch spread peanut butter on a cracker and carefully patted it down with his knife seven times.

"He's cowboy crazy," Lisbeth said. "But he'll be feeding the geese at Flat Willow."

Petch winked at me. "Doesn't want to move?" He held his cracker in mid-air. He had a deep and pleasant voice; its smoothness made me think of cherry-flavoured medicine slipping down my throat.

"He'll get over the cows," my father said.

Petch lowered the hand with the cracker and talked very thoughtfully in his deep voice. It was almost spooky that he should have such a low voice, for he wasn't a big man at all. "Well, when you consider the apostle he's named after," he said, "you can hardly blame him for being stubborn. But you know, an apple, when it falls to the ground, doesn't land far from the tree."

Everybody was silent.

"Dad's a riddle man," Christoph said.

"That's no riddle," Sara spoke up. She was smart about things like that.

"Aha, girl!" Petch raised the hand with the cracker. "But it is."

Sara shook her head, giving Petch a challenging look.

"Think girl, think sharp," Petch laughed. He lowered the hand with the cracker and picked up some peanut butter with his knife. He patted it down on the cracker, over and over.

Olvetter tapped his cup with a spoon. "Here's another one to think about," he said. "If you want the apple tree to grow up straight, when's the best time to tie it to the post? When it's young or when it's old?"

Petch winked at me, and at that moment his overloaded cracker snapped in two and fell into his coffee. Everybody schmutzled a little. I stifled a laugh. "Petch, when's the best time to eat your cracker?" I wanted to say.

Chapter Three

After dinner on Thursday, the German schoolteacher drove Old Schimbel around the kuchel, and tooted the horn. My married sister Dorothea, who had stayed behind when the others had gone to Saskatchewan on Monday, called us together, and Anna and Judy and I joined the lineup at the bus. The seats filled quickly. Dorothea said we'd sit in the back seat. As we sat down, I saw Ronni Kleinser and his brother Davi step onto the bus. Ronni chased two smaller boys off a seat and he and his brother plopped themselves down on it. I clenched my teeth. Those two were just like their father, the pigman.

My cousin Maria was in the crowd outside. Her little brothers reached toward the bus and tried to wriggle free from her hands. I watched Maria out of the corner of my eyes, thinking what a rabbit I'd been. I'd had plenty of chances. Especially since after lotday, when I'd helped Katrina-Pasel unpack the Hufer family's boxes. I could easily have done it behind the boxes when nobody was around if I weren't such a chicken. How long could it have taken, anyway, to give her a kiss? One second? Five seconds? But all I had done was talk about school things, about drawing, about the cows, and about Flat Willow. Think and act serious. I did a lot of that.

Dorothea poked me with her elbow. "Aren't you at all excited about Flat Willow?"

I shrugged, then fiddled with the yellow envelope I had brought with me. My sister fluffed her pillow and made herself comfortable. "You know, mules have a hard road," she said.

"Well then, let's travel," the teacher called out over all the noise in the bus.

On the way out of Rockyview, we passed the old cowbarn. At the corral gate stood Madeline, and beside her, the only cowboy of Rockyview — my lost comrade Hufer Miechel. He waved. I raised my hand just a little, and turned aside. Dorothea noticed, and took hold of me, hugging me against herself, right into the plumpness of her stomach. She was warm and smelled of powder.

"Weep yourself happy." I heard her muffled voice over the road noise. Then suddenly I felt it. A kick. Right against my face. I pulled up quickly. Dorothea's hand flew over her mouth to hide a smile. "It's a good sign," she said.

I didn't open my envelope till Old Schimbel whined down at the crooked sign that said "Fort Macleod 23 KM." By then, Rockyview had long disappeared behind the foothills. My envelope held the one thing that no person in the world could take away from me. My family could've moved to the moon, but I'd still have The Cowboy Kid. He came from inside my head.

I had a thing about westerns. When I drew, I thirsted for orange pop. So did The Cowboy Kid. In my very first story, the cowboy spent three days in the desert, without water. Boy, he was thirsty! That evening my mother opened a big bottle of Orange Crush, and the satisfaction went straight to my head, and The Cowboy Kid's head too.

I decided not to draw on the bus. Anna and Judy already knew not to tell, and Dorothea just smiled and said I was a good drawer. But if the wrong person looked back and saw The Cowboy Kid, the German schoolteacher would soon find out. "Gunfighting books do not belong in a peaceful community," he lectured us once when he punished the grade seven boys with a leather strap for reading Louis L'Amour pocketbooks.

While the wheels underneath sang on the highway, I planned The Cowboy Kid's next move. I was the boss. The bad guys had no chance. They were usually fat boozers like Kleinser

Chuck, the pigman. I'd hated the pigman for a long time. He was brother to Dorothea's man Thom, but I didn't care. The way I figured, he deserved to be hated. It wasn't *me* who had walked up behind *him* in the pigbarn once and given him a shock on the rear with a stock prod and laughed about it in his face. He'd done it to me. I'd been in the pigbarns only two times at Rockyview, and each time he'd done something that made me hate him.

In the last square, The Cowboy Kid was camping for the night. He was headed for Gulch Rock to stop the whiskey-drinking outlaws from robbing the Lone Shark Bank. "Those outlaws sure have a surprise coming!" the balloon caption said. The Kid thought the stars above were good souls smiling down from heaven. He had a cactus fire going and was heating a can of beans and brewing a cup of cowboy coffee — coffee so black and thick, you could float a horseshoe in it. I knew he would have liked to pack a case of orange pop, but in the Old West a cowboy had to be tough. He'd wait. Once the outlaws were locked in the town jail, he would use some of the reward money to buy three bottles of Orange Crush at a pop machine in the Gulch Rock Hotel. And he would sit in the bar and quench his thirst. He would go burp...burp...burp, one burp for each bottle. After that he would have a meal of fried perogies and swine wurst, play poker with the sheriff, then go to bed.

* * * *

The foothills settled into the rolling prairie. The towns along the Number Three highway rose up and grain elevators sailed by, then, like the mountains, shrank into the horizon. People of the world, the English, whooshed by in cars and vans and trucks. I made myself tiny in the seat. I knew that many of them hated the Gmanshofter and didn't want to give us any more land. They hated the communal people like the Catholics had hated Jakob Hutter in the Old Country, and like the Russians had hated the forebears and tried to pull them into the war when they lived in Russia. People told rumours about the Gmanshofter, rumours that weren't true. They thought we were planning to build more and more colonies and buy up all the land. Olvetter had warned us. The Bible told about how evil the world would be near the end. That's why Gmanshofter were supposed to be careful. We didn't mix with people on the broad road of sin because of the great danger that they'd pull us along too.

Somewhere between Medicine Hat and Maple Creek my eyelids got heavy and I drifted back to Rockyview. Hufer Miechel and I were riding Madeline in the foothills. We came to a hill with doors at the sides. I tried to push Hufer Miechel off Madeline first and he tried to push me off first. Suddenly a man with piercing eyes and a flat forehead charged out the wide door. He moaned, and made slapping sounds as he walked. With a gleam in his dark eyes, he ran toward us. Before I could kick Madeline to a gallop, the retarded man had yanked me off Madeline and was shaking me.

Then I realized it was Anna who was shaking me. "We just drove into Saskatchewan," she said. I rubbed my eyes and shook my head to make sure I was awake. I was sweating. Some of the windows were wide open because of the heat, and the curtains were flapping like mad.

"Where? Where?" Judy reached across Anna's lap and pulled Dorothea's hand from her knitting. "Where is it? I can't see it," she said. Dorothea smiled and said nothing.

I touched Dorothea's arm. "Do you think dreams ever come true?"

"What's wrong now?"

"I had that dream again, where the poor man came out of a rootcellar and tried to kill me."

Dorothea straightened my katus and shook her head. "Haven't you forgotten about that one yet?" she said, twirling more wool around her finger.

I watched the land move by for a long time, and got tired

of watching for cows in the hills that came and went between stretches of green and golden grain fields. The endless whine of Old Schimbel's wheels on the highway and the little fans whirring up front lulled me back and forth from the bus to Rockyview, and Flat Willow too. As in the pictures I'd seen, I saw the long belt of naked trees, the drifts of snow and the rib-like frames of the unfinished unithouses. The wind wailed like wolves. A coulee twisted away into the depths of a storm.

I awoke with a jump. Anna was shaking me again. "We turned off the highway, Peter," she said. A sour smell filled my nose and my forehead was sticky. I jerked and my hands flew in front of me. Up front, a little school kid with a dazed look was puking into a syrup pail.

The teacher was talking. "You'll see the roof of an old shack looking out over some willow scrubs at the side of a coulee," he said. "Don't mind the shack, it's nothing. Look east, past the coulee, past that long shelterbelt there. Flat Willow sits on the other side, on the flatland."

A woman spoke up above the loud cheers of the children. "Tell us, schoolteacher. Is that the coulee where that poor man died?"

"Yes," the teacher said, glancing back.

Beside me, Dorothea suddenly let her knitting drop into her sewing bag, and she sat up straight.

"And is it true what the builders said about him, schoolteacher?" the woman asked. "Did he really tame the pigs?"

I saw the teacher's face in the rearview mirror. "That's what *they* said." His grin went to one side of his face. "But you know how little you can believe *some* people."

Dorothea's nostrils twitched, and she stared into space without blinking. "Will people be talking about this till the end of the world?" she said quietly. "Why can't they leave the past where it belongs?"

I waited for a minute before I spoke. "Dorothea. What

did Thom say? Did he believe the gun disappearing and the poor man freezing to death were connected?"

Dorothea gave me a impatient look. "Those incidents were almost six months apart," she said. "Only a loosewit would believe there was anything to it. So just be quiet about it. It's dead and buried. Let it rest."

I wasn't sure it was buried. People were always bringing it up.

Shortly, we sighted Flat Willow. The little children bounced and slid about on the vinyl seats, flapping their hands with great excitement. A jackrabbit shot from the grass in the ditch. Moments later I saw an English girl, walking at the coulee edge. She was too far away for me to see her face, but I saw she wore a bright green cap, and her light hair hung out the back in a pony-tail. About half a mile to the south, beside some low hills, stood the shack.

"The neighbour's girl...," I heard the teacher say over the noise on the bus. I turned to peer out the rear window, and my eyes stayed on the girl until Old Schimbel turned to follow a bend in the road.

Chapter Four

The road to Flat Willow followed the coulee and wandered in dizzy curves and rises like my brother's trail went when he lifted the bottle too often. But at the truck scale and a grandiose range of silvery granaries and tall white bins, it made one last curve and got straight. In front of three enormous yellow buildings with low-pitched roofs and windowless garage doors, it broadened into a bay-like road topped with pale crushed rock. Then it forked into tire-track lanes, which continued alongside four unithouses that sat on both sides of the kuchel. All the buildings there had sky blue clapboard siding on the bottom third, and white siding on top.

We all stared in awe; hardly anybody spoke. The builders who had built up Flat Willow over the two years had boasted plenty when they came home to visit every two weeks. The ground was still barren: there were no trees, lawns or permanent walkways yet — just a few planks laid across mud patches here and there. Still, it was a grand place.

The teacher drove Old Schimbel down the middle road and parked at the kuchel. At the south end of the building, the road turned completely around and went back out on the other side. Where it looped, a footpath topped with crushed rock continued toward the big school, widening, as if to pause for a moment, at a little building that was, the teacher said, the shoeshop and boiler house.

As we stepped off the bus, people who had already

arrived on Monday came from all corners to greet us. My mother huffed up too, smiling like a cherub. Her work skirt and bodice, and the old-style button shoes she wore, were splotched with white paint.

"God be thanked, you made it," she said.

Later, after we'd had a late supper in the dining hall, my mother told me I should go and look in at Olvetter's. I was glad to go. Although the awning windows were cranked all the way open, the rooms my sisters worked in were a turpentine hell. They had stripped the varnish off some old chests. The fumes of the fresh varnish made my eyes water and my nose burn.

"Just don't go groaning about Rockyview," my mother called after me.

My grandfather lived in an unfinished unit while my mother and her crew prepared our units. The walls and floor of his temporary room were bare, with just plywood. He was in the southernmost room of the entire house. Near the door stood his leatherette upholstered bench for the visitors, and two old chairs. His antique wall-cabinet leaned, empty, against a corner. On the opposite wall hung his Swift thermometer and his wall clock, and someone had also hung his bookshelf for him, which held several thick black books. The room smelled of new wood and the lingering scent of Sara's rose perfume. Sometimes my sisters had no measure. I thought they practically poured the stuff on themselves.

Olvetter was reading his Bible with a magnifying glass; a funnel-shaped table lamp flooded the pages with yellow light. I stood for a moment in the doorway before the old man looked up. His wall clock ticked to the rhythm of the shiny pendulum behind the glass. Olvetter turned a page, then laid his magnifying glass on the pages. He looked up and smiled. "Well, well," he said. "Now, here you are. In Saskatchewan."

My eyes were on his antique field glasses on the table. "Do you see much out there?" I asked.

Olvetter motioned for me to pick them up.

The sun made me squint. It was just beginning to slip into orange-smeared cloud pockets hanging low over the shelterbelt. The pale yellow siding of the barns stood out sharply against the shelterbelt in the back. Across a rut-road far to the south, erected by poles and a metal frame, a cement mixing tank pointed to the sky. Everywhere else was a swell of pasture land. A pair of dark birds swooped across my view to the old shack sitting at the coulee edge, then vanished behind the shelterbelt.

I swung the binoculars back to the barns.

"Why don't we have cattle, Olvetter?" I asked. There was one small corral beside a little barn hardly bigger than the shoeshop. My father had told me before supper that Flat Willow had the grand total of four dairy cows and five steers — just enough for the community. "Oh wowdy," I had said.

Olvetter pushed away his Bible. "There is no quota — you know that."

"I mean range cattle. There is so much land. We could build a real corral."

His chair creaked. "You're a smart boy, you understand things." He leaned forward and lowered his voice. "See the pigbarns out there? That's the biggest operation in colonies from the Rocky Mountains down to South Dakota.

"When I was young like you — but my heavens we were poor — we had everything. We had grain, swine, cows and horses, sheep, turkeys, geese, ducks. But nowadays communities don't build like that."

"Why not?"

"The world is verruckt, that's why. And we follow. It's out of control, chasing the dollar. Just like" — he thumped his Bible — "God spoke it. It's all clear, the end's for sure on the doorstep."

"But cattle is big market," I said.

The old man seemed irritated. "For sure it's big market, but since we have no range land nor dairy — " Someone had come into the house through the main door. It was Sara.

"Olvetter, why didn't you come lunch with us?" she said. "Here, I brought you some strawberry pie." She set the plate on the table and left as quickly as she had come.

I swung the binoculars back and forth a few times, then focussed on the shack, which was getting dark in the fading light. "Is that shack ours?" I asked.

He yawned. "Our land stops at the coulee."

"What about the shack, though?"

"I can't tell you for sure. But I'll be your prophet it won't be left alone. Some people these days don't appreciate old buildings."

I moved the glasses right and left a few more times. When I turned to lay them down, I saw that the old man had fallen asleep in his chair.

* * * *

I woke up to the song "Alone and Yet Not All Alone." The clock was almost half-to-seven. My parents were singing their devotions in the next room. Beside me, Jake rolled over. He blinked hard, then pulled his pillow over his head to shield himself from the morning. I lay back and stared at the grain on the plywood ceiling. Sara had teased me before bedtime: "Some day you'll find yourself a girlfriend, get baptised and married, and live with her in this very unit." I had snorted at the idea.

A wedge of sunlight streaked across the wall and the singing stopped.

"Gut Morng, Josh," my mother said.

"Rebekah, send your son Pete down to the goosebarn pronto after breakfast," Josh-Vetter said in English. One of my uncle's quirks was that he spoke English most of the time. But, as hard as he tried to talk sophisticated, he still spoke half Deitch and holber English.

He left right away, and my parents resumed their singing. They always sang. Before breakfast they sang morgen lieder, and at night they sang abend lieder. My father had a firm voice, but it took wrong turns sometimes. My mother's high-pitched and wavery voice kept their singing on the road, because she knew the melodies. I couldn't imagine my father singing alone when he went to the field before breakfast. His voice belonged with my mother's like the thick black cover of our Bible belonged with the soft pages inside. The songs, which the forebears sang in the Old Country, often terrified me, yet they also made me happy. They were mostly about death, about eternal bliss for pious people, but also about the eternal pain of evil people, those whom God would damn to hell. We were lucky to have the songs. That's what the German schoolteacher said. The more fervour you sang them with, the more strength God gave you to push down sin and the lust of the flesh. That fleishes lust. That, and your free will, could get you into a lot of trouble. I sang with my parents only on Saturday evenings in the winter. But I had made a vow to myself that someday — not today, mind you — but someday before I died, I would become extremely religious. And I would yet save my soul from getting damned to hell forever and ever. Maybe when I got baptised, maybe sooner, but the day would come when I would start singing the songs day and night, and read the Bible every day.

The bell on the roofpeak of the kuchel rang for the adults, and I got up to dress. Jake and Petch's boys from Moon Ranch were still sleeping. Most of the teenagers who were out of school already didn't go to the kuchel for breakfast. They counted on lunch at half-to-nine.

* * * *

The goose yard was a noisy place. The geese greeted me at the farm fence up front, half running, half flying. They landed a few feet in front of the gate, chattering and beating their clipped wings. Some hissed. I wasn't sure if they were glad to see me or if they were getting ready to attack. I stood for a moment at the gate. Then I shoved my hands through the air to clear a path.

"Stupid devils," I said.

The yard had four sections, arranged so the barn stood in the centre. My uncle was in the midst of a feeding frenzy in the section that held the ducks. Hundreds of ducks shovelled down their breakfast like maniacs. They scooped more than their beaks held, and jerked their heads back to shake the feed down their throats. Josh-Vetter leaned against a water hydrant; an arc of water flowed from a hose in his hand. Wet feed was probably easier for the dumbheads to gulp down.

"Ah, my helper," the gooseman said.

I shrugged.

Josh-Vetter peered over the top of his glasses. He had weird-looking glasses. The frames were sort of egg-shaped and were thick and heavy. And they were black like his beard, which was just a thin strip that followed the edges of his square jaw. When he spoke, he sounded as if his nose was plugged up.

"Now, Pete, don't think that you're the only one who feels displaced." He launched into a sermon right away. "We all have a special place in our hearts for the old colony. Do you think *I* wanted to come here and be a gooseman? Do you think *I* wanted to become a shoemaker? But that's our way. We do the community's bidding whether we want to or not."

Maybe you will also become the next preacher. Out loud I said, "I'm okay, Josh-Vetter. I don't give a hoot about Rockyview any more." But I looked at my feet when I said it.

Josh-Vetter was in a hurry to get back to the work in his house. He explained my duties. I was to fill the feed troughs twice a day with barley chop, make sure the water troughs had water in them, and make absolutely sure the gates were closed.

"It's a soft job," he said. "A retarded man could do it."

I agreed. The job was as easy as farting in the wind.

"Sorry to rush off, Pete, but I gotta keep up with everyone else," my uncle said, and he lumbered off.

I explored the barn. There was nothing unusual about it: unpainted plywood walls and ceilings, a dirt floor in two of the three sections, and windows with lots of cobwebs. Brooders hung near the ceiling from cables attached to winches. The ducks and geese had lived here when they were small, but now it stood empty. And it smelled of old manure, and cigarettes. Someone was using the goosebarn for a smoking hideout.

I tugged at the leather strap clasped to my suspenders and pulled my watch from my pants. I still had plenty of time till half-to-nine lunch. Why not be the first of the boys to explore the coulee behind the shelterbelt?

As I stepped through the thick shelterbelt, the drone of the exhaust fans at the pigbarns faded away. Goosebumps pricked up on my skin. It was cool there, and the air smelled of grass and leaves and old rain. The sun hadn't wheeled high enough yet to heat the west side. But the chill wasn't just from the sudden shade. There was something spooky about slipping behind a wall of thick willows. The ability to vanish from every eye in the community in the swish of a cow's tail was at once comforting and scary. If a person were inclined — which I wasn't — to sneak around a lot, why, he could easily sneak off without anybody knowing. Lord, it was almost a shame I wasn't such a person, for who knew how far that coulee went.

But just as quick, thoughts about the dead man and the stolen gun came into my head. That was the trouble with being an artist. An artist could imagine things completely easy. The dead man lay frozen in the snow, his face horrible, blue and stiff. I pushed the vision into a deep rootcellar. It floated back through a crack in the door, so I dumped a wagonload of straw bales there. I clenched my fist to give me courage.

I managed to keep the dead man in the rootcellar, and stooped to go through the barbed-wire fence. At the bottom of the coulee, bordered by cattails and reeds, was a slough. Wild ducks made circles in the water. Near the slough, sun-bleached foxtails danced in the breeze.

"*Conkeree, conkeree.*" Red-winged blackbirds screeched in the wild rosebushes at the side of the coulee. I jumped. Then, three minutes later, as I made my way through half-dead Russian thistles, something shot from the grass in front of me. My heart almost turned a somersault. Cottenpicken' rabbit! Lord, I was jumpy.

As I neared the shack, a breeze fanned my back. Then I heard the music. I stopped abruptly and crouched down behind a rosebush, my heart thumping in my ears. It was a clanging sound, as if someone were tcheipering around with a bunch of copper pipes inside an empty granary. There was no melody, just *tinkle tinkle tinkle*. I was still about a hundred feet from the shack and I couldn't see what was making the music. The shack was a gray old thing with a shake roof, and there wasn't a hint of paint on it. It had probably rotted off many years ago, or had been pelted off by the rain, ripped off by the wind, or frozen off by the cold.

Then suddenly I saw a head pass by a knocked-out window in the shack. Seconds later, the English girl appeared in the doorway. In her hand she held a pocketbook. What was she doing here? Was I trespassing on the neighbour's land?

The girl walked to a lichen-covered boulder near the shack and hoisted herself up, and sat with her back toward me. She wore a white T-shirt with orange stripes, and blue jeans. Her hair, the colour of butterscotch, was long and wild, as if whipped by the wind. She opened her book and flipped some pages. I craned my neck, but heard only the tinkly sound.

I thought about it later, how, when a rabbit leaps up in front of you in the grass, it tears off like a rocket, then stops at a safe distance to look back. That's what I did. I dodged behind willow scrubs and rosebushes, and made my way back to the shelterbelt. I kicked at the grass tufts in front of me. The boys would laugh if they knew. "Wolner Peter the chicken, ran from a girl," they would say. Jake would laugh like a maniac. And my sisters would tease me.

I checked my watch. It was almost half-to-nine lunch. There was no use turning back now. Coffee and rhubarb stritzel would be waiting at home. I'd seen Sara carry the pan home from the kuchel earlier. I never missed the opportunity to eat rhubarb stritzel.

"The girl wouldn't have been friendly, anyway," I said out loud. "She's just an English girl, and who cares about the English people? They hate the Gmanshofter."

At the shelterbelt I stood and looked back for a long time. The roof of the shack peeked over the top of the willows.

Chapter Five

The gardenboys had a hankering to catch the first batch of gophers at Flat Willow. Ronni Kleinser brought it up at the table, and in the swish of a cow's tail I wanted to go too. Ronni's brother Paul and Eddie Wipf, who sat at the end of the long table where the coffee kettles stood, made smirk-faces and said catching gophers for jawbreakers was as stupid as borscht for breakfast. They were the seventh graders — you couldn't talk to them any more. Ronni placed his hands near the sides of his head when the German teacher wasn't looking, and we had a quick laugh. He was mimicking a teenager so close to fourteen and a member of the adults that his head had already swelled up to fill in the styled black hat he'd be wearing soon. You'd have never caught me making that sign with those tough guys so near. But Ronni wasn't afraid of anybody.

"Is he still giving jawbreakers?" Jerg Wipf ignored Paul and Eddie.

Ronni forked more cottage cheese perogies onto his plate and spooned a patch of fruit moos overtop. "Why wouldn't he?" he said.

"I don't care about the jawbreakers," I said.

Ronni gave me a strange look. "You don't care about the jawbreakers?"

"I just want to catch the gophers."

"But it's the jawbreakers why we go after 'em."

"Is it really?"

Ronni scowled. "You know what you are, Wolner Peter?"

"What?"

"You're a smart aleck."

I just grinned.

Ronni's younger brother Davi touched my arm. "Tell us about the time Hufer Miechel cut gopher tails in half to cheat the hauswirt."

"No way, not here," I said. The German schoolteacher wasn't far off. He was pacing the floor at the girls' table, and would saunter over to our table soon enough. During a meal he strolled back and forth across the tile floor about ten times. His eyes never strayed far, and his ears were always in range. The women washing the adults' dishes at the big stainless steel sinks outside in the kitchen area made plenty of noise to cover my voice. But I knew the boys. They would laugh out loud. The teacher had a strap in a drawer of the bread table, and he used it on anybody who got too loud.

After dinner I went searching for my gopher trap. My mother was in a cranky mood. She and my sisters were painting walls, and it was very hot in the house.

"Listen, I have no time to spring right loose and go looking for your trap," she said. "You know where your box is. And don't go messing in the other boxes."

It took me ten minutes to dig out my trap. Petch and his sons had stacked the boxes into a corner of an unfinished basement room. I paused to look at my belongings. I didn't own much. Nobody did. "We own nothing to speak of, yet we're all millionaires," my uncle Dan once told me. "Now ain't that a good deal?"

I didn't understand my uncle's logic. I would have liked to own a pair of slick cowboy boots like Jake's, a horse — and an airplane. I smiled when I thought about the airplane. My goodness, it would be handy at Flat Willow. I would fly back to Rockyview on Sunday afternoon while people took their naps.

And I would pick up Hufer Maria at the usual secret place. "Oh wow, you have an airplane now," she'd say. And we'd go for a quick trip to Flat Willow. Actually, I'd need a supersonic jet now, because the airplane wouldn't make it back for Sunday School at half-to-three. But we'd fly over Flat Willow anyway, drink pop and laugh because nobody would know it was us. She would sit real close to me and watch me work the fancy instruments, which I would have invented because I would be an inventor and have a special place underground somewhere, where I'd invent all kinds of machines and telephones and stuff. And I would put the jet on automatic pilot like Tom Swift did in the Tom Swift books. Then Hufer Maria and I would go to the back where I would draw The Cowboy Kid for a while. And she'd lean over my shoulder....

I closed the box. All I had was my Number 1 trap, a paper kite, a stack of western comic books — which I kept secretly — a wooden sled that Olvetter and I had nailed together in the woodworking shop at Rockyview, pencils and pens, my German Testament and hymn-books. It was no use thinking about Hufer Maria any more. She was hundreds of miles away. Just like everything else at Rockyview.

* * * *

It was always more fun drowning out the gophers. The traps made it too easy. We'd pour slough water down the hole and keep pouring till the gopher, wet and goggle-eyed, came up. When it tried to run to another hole, we were behind its tail with our big sticks. One bang on the head was all a gopher took.

But there weren't any gopher holes near the slough.

"Maybe there aren't any gophers in Saskatchewan," Ronni Kleinser said.

"We're just not in the right place," I said.

"Maybe the winters are too cold here," Jerg Wipf said. "That's why that poor man froze, you know."

Nobody spoke for a minute. Ronni's face twitched.

I turned to Jerg Wipf. "What has that got to do with it?"

"He froze," Jerg said.

"But he walked out into a blizzard," I said. "Gophers hibernate."

Ronni picked up his trap and waterpail and started walking away. "Shut up about that dumb man already," he said. "Nobody wants to hear about him any more." He pointed to the shack. "I'm going to explore that shack."

I thought about the English girl then. "It's not on our land," I said. "It's the neighbour's."

"It's just a useless old shack," Ronni said.

One of gardenboys, Jerg Wipf's little brother, tugged at my arm. "Wolner Peter, stay and tell us how Hufer Miechel tried to cheat the hauswirt with gopher tails."

"Not now, Levi. I want to see the shack too."

Ronni stopped. "Tell it on the way."

"Och, you don't really want to hear it. It's so old, it's got beards already."

"You liar. We know how much you like telling the story. You don't have to pretend," Ronni said.

"Okay," I said, picking up my trap at the side of a badger hole. "I guess you buggers nagged me into telling it."

I always talked in English when I told the story, the way I imagined a storyteller should. If I could've imitated Petch, with his smooth voice, I would have had the world by the tail.

"Well, me and Mike Hofer and John Kleinsasser and Johnny Wurz were looking for gophers at Rockyview...you know...out in the foothills by the red feed bin...where the grass is so low all the gophers had to move to Montana — "

"It was not," Jerg Wipf cut in, spoiling my concentration. "It was in the other one, nearer to the mountains."

"Shut up, George," Ronni also spoke English. "For all we care, it could've been on the damn moon."

I continued in my special voice. "Okay...as you

blockheads know...." I knew I could get away with calling the boys blockheads when I told my story. I called Ronni a son-of-a-pigman once. It was true. He was the pigman's son. But he didn't like the way it sounded and wrestled me to the ground and gave me a few punches in the head. But I wasn't afraid of the other gardenboys.

I continued. For good measure I started at the beginning. "As you blockheads know, back at Rockyview the boss used to give us a jawbreaker for every gopher tail we brought him. Now, one day out there in the foothills where the *red bin* stands, we had about as much luck catching gophers as a gold digger in a manure pile" — I watched the boys' faces — "but dammit, we wanted jawbreakers. We'd carried I don't know how many damn pails of water from the creek up to the hill to drown out the gophers, but their holes were deep and drank gallons and gallons of water...."

The boys were laughing already. They loved it when I swore like a Turk to pepper the story up a little. I side-stepped a rosebush and continued.

"Well, as we were walking home, we counted up the tails. All we had was four lousy tails. One jawbreaker each for all that work. Then Mike Hofer got the idea to cut the tails in half so we'd get two jawbreakers each. We all laughed and said Mike was a genius. That dumb old boss wouldn't catch on in a hundred years. So we laid the tails on a rock and cut them into halves with my pocket knife.

"We were almost home when Mike said maybe we could go for four jawbreakers each if we cut the tails just once more.

"'I don't know if that's a good idea,' we said. But Mike bugged us till we all said okay, let's do it. So out came the knife on another rock."

"What happened next?" Levi asked.

"Well, wait, sonny boy. So we walked into the boss's office and gave him all those gopher tails.

"'Hhhhmmmm,' the boss said. You know how he looks

over his glasses and stares like an owl. 'Damn, it must have been a cold winter,' he said. 'These poor gophers plumb froze their tails off but for a little stub.'"

Jerg Wipf cut in again. "The hauswirt wouldn't say 'damn'."

"George, say one more word and...," Ronni warned.

I frowned at both Jerg Wipf and Ronni, and tried to get back my concentration.

"So anyway, the boss said, 'These cottonpicken' gophers damn near froze their tails off but for a little stub.'

"'Oh, for sure,' we said.

"'Well, well,' the boss said over and over. He pulled a measuring tape from a drawer. And he laid the tails on the table. He measured them this way and that way. Then he pulled a bag from the drawer. And he shook the tails from the bag and made a pile beside the stubby tails. He held one tail up to the window light and you could see it was real bushy and almost three inches long.

"'These are the tails you brought me two days ago,' he said. 'Now why do you suppose these tails you brought today are so much shorter?'

"'Because it was a cold winter,' Mike Hofer said.

"'But tell me this, little boy,' the boss said. 'Did the long-tailed gophers fly south then, where it was warmer?'

"And you know what the dumbhead said?"

The boys shook their heads, pretending they didn't know.

"That Mike. He looked up, and he had his eyes on the jar of jawbreakers on the shelf, and he said, 'Yeah, I guess so.'"

The boys slapped their knees and we all laughed like regular heathens.

By now we were a mere hundred feet from the shack. I kept looking to see if the girl was still there, but I couldn't see her.

"Did you get any jawbreakers, Wolner Peter?" Levi asked.

"I'll let you be the judge about that," I said.

"You sure tell the story good, Wolner Peter," Levi said, sidling up to me and pulling at my hand.

I grinned. The way I figured, I was the best storyteller at Flat Willow. And I was loaded with pride about that.

Ronni stopped abruptly. He held up his hand. "Did you hear that?" he whispered.

We listened. I heard it then. It was the same tinkly music that I'd heard in the morning. Ronni started running first, and we all followed. Jerg Wipf was the first to reach the shack. He burst into the doorway, and the rest of us were right behind him.

Loose boards were scattered topsy-turvy on the floor of the shack. It smelled like old cobwebs and bird dirt.

"Where the devil is it coming from, anyway?" Ronni shouted. "I can't see bugger all."

A pair of barn swallows fluttered past our heads. Ronni swore and picked up a stick. He whacked at some boards propped against the wall, then at a stack of chalkboard pieces that leaned to the side like Jake at Sunday morning church. He kicked at it, and the whole stack crashed to the wooden floor. Jerg Wipf stepped over the mess and bounded across the room toward a white cupboard sitting in a corner.

"We shouldn't wreck things," I said. "I think this shack belongs to the neighbour. I saw an English girl here this morning."

"You liar," Ronni said.

"I did. It was the neighbour's girl."

"Stop lying. What would a girl do here?"

I glared at Ronni. I knew he'd wrestle me to the ground and beat me up if I tried anything. He had muscles as strong as hydraulics. He was also the oldest of the garden crew, and they worshipped him. All except Jerg. He was an oddball. And he was like me: serious and stubborn about certain things. But if Ronni told any of the others to set fire to the shack, they'd probably do it. It was just an old shack, but I knew how my grandfather felt about old buildings, and I couldn't see any sense in demolishing it.

CRASH. Davi had an old broom in his hand and had shattered one of the four window panes. Ronni joined in. CRASH. Another pane was gone. Then the third. And the fourth.

Then Jerg Wipf found the books. "Look what I found," he called out. He stood at the old cupboard, balancing a stack of books about a foot high in his hand.

Ronni Kleinser dashed to his side. "Give 'em here," he said.

"No way. I saw them first."

Ronni shoved Jerg against the wall and the books tumbled from his hands. I leaped forward and managed to rescue four of the books.

But Ronni got most of them. "Hah," he gloated. "They'll be worth money in the city."

Jerg glowered at Ronni, and gritted his teeth. He always got the short end when Ronni was around. All he had was one book. "No, you blockhead, don't go after him, he'll beat you up," I wanted to cry out. But I said nothing.

A sly grin came over Jerg's face. He looked past Ronni, past the broken windows. He shoved his fist into his pocket, and fingered something inside. Suddenly he threw the book to the floor and scurried out the door.

Ronni laughed. "He's going home to his mamma now."

Jerg's head passed by the knocked-out window. For a minute nobody spoke. Then we heard the tinkly sound. We all dashed out the door. But Jerg was running for home by the time we got to the side of the shack. A piece of cut rope dangled from the eaves. Under Jerg's arm a bunch of loose brass pipes were tcheipering away.

I looked at Ronni. He had a glare on his face. I bit my tongue, careful not to grin too much. Nobody ever beat Jerg Wipf in a race.

Chapter Six

I had always worked in the summer. Even at six years old, I had worked in the fifteen-acre garden at Rockyview Colony with the German schoolteacher and his crew. Wherever there was communal work, like stacking bales on the haystack during haying season or pounding nails somewhere, you were expected to show up if you had nothing else to do. It felt good to be there, even if you had to just stand around because the top of the haystack had so many men and boys on it that it looked like an anthill. But people who just sat around on their rears and sought ways to weasel themselves out of the work, unless they were ill or had a sore back, were useless sandbags or lazy dogs.

My mother said she had work for me in the house when I wasn't *busy* with the geese. That I was sort of a sinner, I knew. What with the cursing I did, and lying like the devil underfoot, I knew the day couldn't be far off when I'd turn myself around and become extremely religious. But a lazy dog? No way. Not me. I had every intention to do my share of the work.

But...lazy dog or not, I *did* run off to the goosebarn after supper — without stopping at the house. The geese and ducks scooped water and preened their feathers at the water troughs. I was, after all, the gooseboy. The community had given me a job, and I wasn't the type to do things in a slipshod manner. What if the hose on the water trough popped off suddenly? Wouldn't that cause a flood? Well, in case it happened, I would be there to fix it.

As I did my extremely important duties at the water troughs, my mind was like a seesaw. One minute I was going back to that shack, the next minute I wasn't. My stomach felt like a storm of bees from all that teeter-tottering around in my head.

Before supper I had looked over the four books that I had rescued. They were difficult. At first, I had just flipped through them to see if they had any pictures. One was called *The Pigman*. That seemed interesting. I wondered if he'd be a whiskey-drinker like the pigman of Flat Willow. The next two, I laid aside. *I Heard the Owl Call My Name* didn't interest me. Neither did the one called *Of Mice and Men*. I was like that. If I didn't like the title right away, I wasn't interested. Then there was one called *The Catcher in the Rye*. I started reading a little in that one because it reminded me of Jake out in the rye field at Rockyview. We'd had a rye field outside the school fence. I remembered my first year in English school, when the grade eights, who always bossed the younger kids around, sent Jake to the outfield. But he goofed off most of the time. When a ball soared over the caragana, which wasn't too often, he'd be sitting in the rye, eating the green kernels and reading comics. They kicked him off the team at least once a week. Anyway, the guy in the book — his name was Holden Caulfield — got kicked out of school. But the exciting, yet scary, thing about the book was the swear words. That guy swore like the devil backwards and forwards. It was scary to read the book alone. So I had pretty much decided I'd return the books to the shack. That was the least I could do, considering the English girl would be missing her pipes that tcheipered like music, and the books Ronni had stolen.

I left my water-trough duties, got the books from where I had hidden them in the goosebarn, and a minute later I pushed through the shelterbelt. I stood by the barbed-wire fence for a few minutes. Nothing stirred but the tree swallows flitting about overhead. Sweat trickled down my temples. I fanned my face with my straw hat and jiggled my pants. My clothes were sticky like the devil and I stank like potato kasha. I wished shorts were allowed. I'd heard somewhere that Arabs in Saudi Arabia wore white clothes because the sun's rays bounced off white clothes. And black clothes pulled the rays into you instead of bouncing them off. I hoped we'd never move to Saudi Arabia.

The books started to sweat in my hands too and I thought all that sweat might make the ink come off the covers. But it didn't. I read a little more of *The Catcher in the Rye*. The story was getting interesting, and I wondered what was going to happen to Holden Caulfield. He had flunked a lot of classes. Boy, he must have been stupid. And he also kept right on swearing like a Turk.

"Stop swearing already!" I said, as if he'd hear me. That eased my conscience a little. At least I wasn't approving of it.

Finally, I stooped through the barbed-wire fence. I was a robot, controlled by radio waves coming from the shack. I walked slowly, stopping to watch mallards dip for food on the slough, then huge dragonflies soaring through the air like choppers.

The girl was sitting in the doorway of the shack, her head between her knees. I thought she might be crying, and I stood like a patient cow. I tried clearing my throat. All that came out was a squeak. But her head jerked up and a plastic pop bottle spun from her hand. She looked toward Flat Willow first, then she saw me.

Neither of us spoke for a minute. The English girl lowered her gaze and froze it at the pop bottle in front of her. I figured she was about my age, or maybe older. Her face was red from the sun, and, like Sara's, round and plump. Her hair flowed out the back of a bright green cap perched on top of her head. And she was half-naked, wearing just blue jean shorts with ravelled edges, and a T-shirt with no arms. I suddenly felt strange. I was glad I had a lot of clothes on.

She was the first to speak. "So it was you," she said, and

right away I knew she wasn't friendly. "Why did you steal my wind chimes?"

"I didn't...the...other boys did."

"But you stole my books." Every word was salted with hate.

"I brought some back," I said, holding up the books. Couldn't she at least appreciate that? She stood up and walked toward me, her eyes never leaving mine. She grabbed the books away and hugged them to her chest. I was sure she hated me like the devil. She was probably a Gmanshofter-fiend, and would start mocking me for my black pants and my suspenders soon.

She turned and walked away.

"Hey, girl, I'm sorry about what happened." The words came out sort of choked.

She turned around slowly, biting her lip. "My name is Tessa Longman. What's yours?" Her voice had a sharp edge to it.

"Peter."

"Just Peter?"

"Peter Waldner." What did she need to know my last name for?

"So it really wasn't you who stole my chimes?"

"No."

She held up the books. "Did you read any?"

"Just three chapters in the red one."

"What's it about?"

"A stupid guy who swears a lot. Haven't you read it?"

"I haven't gotten to that one yet."

"Oh."

"I'll lend it to you if you want."

I shook my head.

"Why not?" she asked.

"It's...I dunno...we're not supposed to swear."

"But *The Catcher in the Rye* is a classic. You have to read the classics sooner or later."

"What's classics?"

"Important books that are so great they can't be forgotten."

"Okay," I said, although I had no idea what she was talking about.

She walked up real close to me and put it in my hand. She smelled of suntan lotion. "There," she said, and stepped back a few feet. Without expression, she kept looking at me. "How old are you, anyway?"

"I'll be thirteen in October," I said, pushing the book into my pocket.

"Cool. I'll be thirteen in two weeks," she said, turning toward the big rock. There was something scary about her. She seemed too grown-up, and her eyes seemed cold, lonely. At the rock, she stretched out her legs and jumped up a little to hoist herself to the top. Then she sat, her feet dangling. She reached into her pocket and pulled out a packet of Juicy Fruit gum.

"Want some, Peter Waldner?"

I smiled. "If you're giving me one, I'll take it."

She laughed. "If you're taking it, I'll give you one." And we both laughed. Well, she did. I just smiled.

As I peeled off the wrapper and folded the gum into my mouth, I relaxed. The English girl seemed caught up in the flavour of her gum, and said nothing. She just chewed and chewed with long, lazy bites and wiggled her foot. Then I started chewing too, while tapping my fingers against my right leg. It was quite something. There I was, at an old shack with an English girl, chewing away like a cow. As we chewed in silence, a question pressed against my mind.

"Why do you come here, anyway?" I asked.

The girl leaned back a little and crossed her legs. She smiled. "I like reading here. It's real cool" — she made a sweep in front of her — "with just the sounds of nature, my wind chimes and an old shack creaking. It's nice, and spooky and all — I don't know — I just like to read."

I couldn't understand why she would want to be spooked, but I could see why she'd want to be alone.

"I like being alone too, to draw westerns," I said.

"About gunfighters?" She seemed surprised.

"I don't make him kill the outlaws. He just makes them bleed a little. He mostly punches them unconscious, then he throws them in jail."

"I thought you people were supposed to be pacifists. My uncle Frank says you are not pacifists."

I felt stupid. "What's pacifists?"

"Don't you know your own history? Pacifists are peaceful people. People who don't believe in guns...." She paused. Some hate had crept back in her voice. "My uncle says the men who built those houses up there — the ones who worked in the pigbarns — they weren't good people."

"How do you mean?"

"They borrowed Mr. Clements' gun to shoot rabbits and blackbirds in the coulee here. You should've seen Pierre. He got mad as thunder."

My scalp crawled and goosebumps pricked up on my skin. I stepped back a few steps. "How do you know about all that stuff?" I asked.

"We used to own the land where your colony sits. And Pierre and I sometimes walked over there to watch the men work. Pierre loved to go to the pigbarns."

"Was he the poor man who froze?"

"Pierre wasn't rich, Peter Waldner, but he sure wasn't poor, either."

"You know what I mean...retarded. Poor in the head."

She laughed nervously. "Your German is funny. Such odd meanings."

My legs seemed to walk off without me. I stared at the rock for a minute. Maybe it was the English neighbours who had started the rumour that the retarded man's death and the stolen gun were connected. The girl must have seen it on my face.

"What's wrong?" she asked.

"Nothing," I lied. I figured the less I told her, the better.

"Did I spook you?" she asked.

I shrugged.

"I'm sorry if I spooked you, Peter Waldner. I didn't mean to."

At that moment the bell at Flat Willow rang. I glanced back. Through a gap in the willows I saw the sun reflecting off my grandfather's window. I tugged at my watch strap to pull my watch from my pants.

"It's the bell," I said, although it was still too early for the bell that meant everybody under fourteen had to go home to their houses.

"I heard it."

"It's...you know...time to go home."

"Oh, you have a curfew."

I said nothing. I didn't like that word. It sounded too much like "coffin". I turned to go.

"Peter?"

"What?"

"I come here every day."

I walked on.

"We could be friends."

I stopped for a moment. Friends with an English girl? Impossible. I kept going.

"Why couldn't we?" She was in front of me suddenly.

This was crazy. A spooky English girl was trying to hold me up.

"Why not, Peter?" she asked. Lord, she was nosey.

"Because you're...."

"A girl?"

"No — well, that too — but you're not from our people," I said. I remembered Jake running to the English neighbour's farm at Rockyview once, to watch movies about a gunfighter named John Wayne. Kleinser Isaac, the preacher, had punished him by making him kneel in the middle of the church floor. I could still see my brother chewing his fingernails as the preacher lectured him in front of the whole community.

"I'll be moving away soon," she said.

I stepped aside to go around her. "I have to go." I looked into her eyes for a moment there, and something inside me wavered. I'd never seen such lonely eyes. Didn't she have someone to talk to? Had she no brothers and sisters? Or cousins? A shiver travelled from the soles of my feet to my scalp.

I walked away and started toward Flat Willow. I looked back a few times as I walked down the coulee. The girl was standing at the rock, staring after me.

Chapter Seven

Sara came to say that coffee and angel food cake were ready in the basement. I sat on a plank laying across two sawhorses, chewing my dead gum with long, serious bites. Lena and Lisbeth stood on the other end. As they painted the ceiling, they talked about boys, and sang hymns. I thought Lonesome Valley should be called Lonesome Coulee.

Sara gave me a funny look. "What ails Peter?"

"Ask him," Lena said. "He's a grouch today."

Lisbeth laughed. "He's just his moody old self."

"What's wrong, Peter?" Sara asked. I knew she'd keep asking questions till she knew everything.

"All I did was ask about what the builders really said about that poor man who froze out there," I said, "and who said that Kleinser Sommel and his brother Joel stole that neighbour's gun."

Sara made big eyes and stepped in front of me. "Why, Peter? Did you see anything?" Her face was very near, and I was afraid she would kiss me. She'd done that the day she turned fourteen: just grabbed me out of the blue and gave me a kiss. Jake had laughed like a maniac and said she was practising for when some boy took her on a date. But Sara was okay. The others often said Sara and I were close, like Anna and Judy were, who were only a year apart. I hardly thought about that. Sara read *The Cowboy Kid* stories. The others just said "wow," but not Sara. When I got lazy with the drawings because I was eager to get to the action part, she knew. "If you draw nothing but action, soon the action gets boring," she'd told me. "And if there's no action at all, it's a poor story." She'd also told me about surprises. "A story has to surprise you, and shock you. Things that make you mad at the bad guys have to happen." She learned all that from reading Nancy Drew mystery books, which the German schoolteacher allowed us to read.

"What happened?" Sara asked for the third time.

"What would have happened?"

"Then why did you ask?"

"I wanted to know what the builders said about the poor man."

"Why did you want to know?"

My mother was painting a windowsill nearby. "Och, Sara, he just needed something to say," she said. "That's why he asked."

"But Mother, didn't people see Ankela's spirit behind the caragana when she died?"

"Some people's eyes are bigger than their head," my mother said.

"Olvetter believed it. Maybe the goosebarn is haunted by that poor man's ghost."

"Sara, don't talk like that. It's a sin."

I heard loud footsteps in the next room and Anna and Judy huffed through the doorway.

"What? Did someone see a spirit?"

My mother placed her paint can on the plank. "Enough of this, let's go lunch."

Anna turned to me. "Tell us, Peter."

"ANNA! Let it rest." My mother gripped my shoulder and steered me out of the room.

"Come with me, Peter," she said. "Help me carry up a few gallons of paint from the storage room. The coffee won't get cold that fast."

We walked on planks zigzagging alongside the unithouse

to the empty unit. My mother walked slowly, breathing heavily. Her hands and arms were splotched white from the paint, and she had a long scab-covered scratch near her elbow, probably from bumping against a sharp nail sticking out somewhere. I winced. Lord, that must have hurt.

"We could've used you this evening." Her voice was plaintive. "There's so much work left. Father is on the field most of the time and Jake helps out in the pigbarn sometimes — Petch's boys are all we have for doing the carpentry. You have a hammer. You could've helped them with the shelves in the coldroom. We have to keep up with the other people."

I felt worse than a wheelbarrow shovelled full of cowpies. Sure, my mother yelled sometimes, but sometimes I wondered if I really deserved to have her. She always stood up for me when my sisters teased me too much, and she was always ready with her sewing machine when my clothes needed a patch, or with a jug of lemonade on a hot day. And in the winter, when the whole family got the flu, my mother hardly ever got sick. She was too busy.

I remembered a certain day back at Rockyview, when I'd thought my mother was dead. I was riding Madeline along a gravel road when I saw a vehicle hurtling toward me. The driver waved his handkerchief out the window of the pickup truck, flagging me down. It was the pigman. "You had better ride home quick, Wolner Peter," he said. "Your mother just fell down the attic, and she's dead." And he roared off like the devil. On the way home the wind whipped my tears as I fiercely kicked and cursed the horse I loved because she wasn't galloping fast enough for me. In my mind I saw everybody standing over the coffin, crying, and people singing the forebears' songs of death at the wake. Although my mother was okay — she hadn't fallen down the attic at all — I'd hated the pigman more than ever from that day on. I'd said over and over that I would always hate him. My hate would be like a snowball. It would grow every time I saw the pigman.

Now, I wanted to tell my mother how glad I was that she was alive, that I loved her, and that I was sorry. But I was like my father. I said nothing.

I should have known there'd be trouble when we walked into the unit. The place stank of pigs. And a light was on downstairs. Someone laughed wickedly. It was Jake. My mother froze right up and stood like a stone.

"Yeah, yeah, you Moon Ranch hounds," my brother slurred from downstairs, "you just ain't got the guts. I could drink you Alberta Hutes under the table every time."

My mother winced.

Then the bad words came. They were dark, and scary. It was nightmarish the way my brother talked when he was drunk. Something inside me shifted. The floor seemed to rise up through me.

My mother trembled and her mouth hung open, as if she'd just hit her elbow against another sharp nail sticking out of the wall. Then her face twisted up. She lifted her paint-splotched apron to her face and her whole body shook from her sobs.

For a moment I stood still. Then I thundered down the steps. My brother had invited the pigman to the storage room for a drink. A forty of whiskey stood half empty on the table. The Moon Ranch boys were standing by, shaking their heads.

"Hey, it's Peter-Vetter," the pigman called out. "Give the boy a drink. Make some hair grow on his chest and toughen him up a little."

I swallowed hard. I couldn't speak. I wished I had a baseball bat. At that moment I wouldn't have thought about being a pacifist.

The pigman had a habit of drinking after work. He could drink down a bottle of whiskey and just burp a little. His stomach, which hung over the top of his pants like two extra stomachs, could easily absorb all the booze. But my brother was just a rookie. That's how Jake said it.

I said nothing. I just ground my teeth together and shot a glare at the two drunks. I started up the stairs. What I wanted to say was unspeakable. And I would never have said it in front of my mother.

"Come, Peter," she called down the stairs. "Hell might lift itself up down there."

As we lunched on angel food cake, Lena and Lisbeth tried to cheer my mother up. They were good at that. With their singing and their talk, they could change the mood so you never would have known something had happened if you hadn't been there. When my father came home from the fields and joined us for coffee, my sisters didn't say a word about Jake. All they talked about was the work. The work, and the progress they'd made. That's how it always was. My father wasn't a talker. He had all those short lines. "Leave it to Jesus." "Just pray." "Everything will pass over." "Every house has its little cross to bear." I wasn't sure everything with Jake would pass over.

My mind was stuck like a fly to syrup the next day. My sisters sang their hymns as they worked. They sang "What a Friend We Have in Jesus" five times. The Moon Ranch boys sang too. Something inside me cried out, and I thought for sure it was my poor soul howling over all my sins. All that swearing I had done, that lying, and running off when my sad mother had needed me. I wasn't any better than Jake. Every time I looked at my mother, I could still see that look of grief that she'd had on her face the night before. What if I became like Jake and got drunk one day and did the same thing?

After chores in the afternoon, I tried reading a little more about Holden Caulfield, but that stupid bugger reminded me so much of Jake, I threw the book against the wall. Then I tried to draw for a few minutes, just to stay in practise. But I couldn't. I felt the cold steel of guns in my brain. I didn't actually feel them — I saw them. The guns were lodged in my brain like the metal wedges you drive into the top of a hammer handle for a snug fit in the hammerhead hole. That gave me a headache. And every time I put my pencil on the paper, I heard the English girl's mocking voice: "You are not pacifists."

I squeezed through the shelterbelt and spied at the shack, then went home again. All those things: the rumours that people told about the Kleinsers, about the man freezing to death in the coulee, that strange English girl, Jake's shocking words, and that swearing Holden Caulfield, made me sick. It was all like a jumble of yarn in my mind.

It got worse. At Sunday morning church, the devil dug at my soul with his sharp claws, and speared me with his fiery branding irons. The preacher talked about how the devil operated. My brain made pictures. First, the devil asks for your finger, making it itch for something you ought not to do. But because you don't know at first that it's the devil who's doing it, you give in. Then he gives you an even bigger desire, and soon he takes your hand too. Once he has your hand, he's in charge. And he directs your foot, so that you walk right into his snares. Even then, the devil tells you lies, smoothing them over with your very own nature, giving you pride and wit. When you finally wake up, the devil's hellish snares are wound around you so severely, you can't move backward or forward.

The longer the preacher talked, the more anxious I felt. The school desk was sticky from my sweat. I turned to look at the people on the pews, first to the women's side, then to the men's side, wondering if they could tell. Everybody's eyes seemed rivetted on me. Up front, near the preacher's desk, the council brethren stared even more. They knew I was a sinner headed straight for hell. The hauswirt stared like Apostle John, Olvetter stared like Prophet Elijah, my father stared like Jesus Christ, and the German teacher stared like Apostle Paul. The only one who didn't stare was Jerg Wipf's grandfather, Speed Jahannes-Vetter, as people called him. His eyes were open just a crack, but he was asleep. He was always asleep.

And I decided. Today I would start being extremely religious. Today I would start singing the forebears' songs every day. And today I would start reading the Testament with fervour. Why put it off to the future? I'd seen how happy my sisters were. Always laughing, always singing. I wanted to have what they had.

A new energy took over me. I shoved the devil into the deep and dark rootcellar, and welded the doors shut. I brought a fleet of payloaders and cement trucks onto the scene and dumped mountains of dirt and cement, closing the devil in that dark place where he belonged. He was probably screaming his head off down there, but that was his tough luck. He'd never get my soul. I would be extremely religious. Even more religious than most people at Flat Willow. I would be pious till death, or till the end of the world. I might not even bother getting married. "I have no time for that," I would tell my sisters. "I have time only for God."

"You fools, are you completely blind?" My mind lectured Ronni Kleinser and the boys at the dinner table. They devoured the broiler chickens and slurped the thin noodles down as if there was no Judgement Day, ever, while I, the gentle and completely pious Gmanshofter, ate with slow, non-violent bites. They talked about ungodly and zeitlicha dinge: gopher tails, killing badgers and skunks, and rummaging through the neighbour's scrap out on the field for copper wire and old beer bottles to make forbidden money with. But my mind was talking to them. "You sinners...you corrupt people...wake up. Come out of that fiery hole and escape from the clutches of the devil. Come, become pious. Save your soul from getting damned to hell forever and ever."

After dinner, I dug my Testament and hymn-books out from the boxes in the basement. I put them in a paper bag and sneaked up the stairs. There was no need to tell my sisters. They'd know it when the power rose up in my eyes. They would never hear another bad word come from my lips. My lips would be good for two things only: singing and praying. And I wouldn't just pray like most people prayed, without a thought to the words. I would pray with such fervour that all the souls in heaven would hear me. In all the colonies, people would say: "Have you heard about Wolner Peter, that boy from Flat Willow?" "Yes, I have. Isn't he the one who is so extremely good?" Hufer Miechel wouldn't believe it. "You, Peter, becoming extremely religious?" "You bet, Miechel. And you too ought to become like me. But do it soon, before it's too late." "And you, Hufer Maria...." Oh, my Lord, my heart was in pain. "Hufer Maria...lieba Hufer Maria...but God has other plans for me, can't you see?"

There was no Sunday School that afternoon. The German schoolteacher said people were too busy. Except for chores, we didn't normally work on Sundays, but the houses had to be finished before harvest. Neither had there been any church in the evenings all week during this busy time. But when you became extremely religious, you didn't wait for church. You were religious before church, during church, and after church. Right up until the day you died.

With my Testament and hymn-books under my arm, I dashed to the goosebarn. I laid open my hymn-books and Testament on the table. And I sang. Lord, I sang. I sang the song "Man Think Daily, Upon Your Mortality." The verses brought tears to my eyes. Electricity seemed to shoot through me. I was too young to be baptised, but that didn't matter to me.

When I finished the song, I was trembling. My Sunday shirt was drenched with sweat. I felt weak, and both hot and cold at the same time. I stepped outside and sat on the cement pad in front of the barn door to dry off. The bright sun made me dizzy. The geese rushed toward me. They could probably see the difference too. As I sat there, I suddenly realized how beautiful the geese were. Their white feathers and their graceful wings were angel-like. And their voices were like the finest singing I had ever heard. The way they held their heads toward the heavens was more beautiful than a scene in the foothills. How could I ever have looked down on such magnificent creatures?

Then I remembered Holden Caulfield. I had put the book into a box on the shelf. What was I to do with the book now that I was extremely religious? Of course. I would have to burn it. No religious person read that vile stuff. I would need to get rid of everything that separated me from God. My westerns and my Cowboy Kid art: everything would have to go.

I stared at *The Catcher in the Rye* for a long time. I would never find out what happened to Holden Caulfield. Too bad. He was a loser anyway. A loser on the road to hell. It served him right.

Footsteps sounded on the cement pad outside. I panicked. I didn't have time to hide. Josh-Vetter walked in. He stopped abrubtly when he saw me.

"What the hell...."

I backed against the table.

"Didn't you see the damn flood out there?" my uncle said. He wore rubber boots and held a screwdriver in his hand. "Jesus, kid," he said. "Are you sure you don't need glasses? Cripes, a blind man would've seen that the hose popped off the water trough out there."

He came closer. I smelled tabbak on his breath. So *he* was the smoker.

"What you standing like that for?" he said. "What are you hiding behind you?"

I didn't know what Josh-Vetter expected to find, but his eyes sure gleamed. As he pushed me aside, he rapped my head with the screwdriver. Lord, it hurt.

"What the Sam Hill?" He snatched up *The Catcher in the Rye*. Then he stared at my Testament and my hymn-book laying open. "You're one strange kid," he said, slipping the book into his pocket. He took a new hose clamp from a box and hurried out the door, shaking his head.

Chapter Eight

Olvetter was the only one who seemed to understand about the hymn-book. "He's starting early," he said. "He might someday be a preacher."

But the others were suspicious. Josh-Vetter told what he'd seen. "Just holding the book in my hand gave me such awful fear that hell was going to tear itself open under my boots," he said. "It was about the most ungodly thing you could imagine. Swear words from cover to cover. I had to pitch it right away into the ash barrel and burn it up. But there Pete was, reading it side by side with the Testament. Be careful with that boy. He might be getting ideas about a different belief in his head."

"You are spending too much time alone," my father warned me on Sunday evening. "People don't mix the martyr's songs and the Testament together with pocketbooks. That's not showing respect for the forebears in the Old Country, who sang those very songs in dungeons to encourage their fellow martyrs and to convert their persecutors to the truth. You have to stop that."

"But Father, I didn't read — "

"Peter!"

"But I was going to — "

"PETER. Don't make me tell you again."

I stayed quiet after that.

My mother backed me into a corner and held me. I

thought she was going to start crying again. "What's become of you, Peter?" she said. "People don't go off to the barns to sing our songs by themselves. They're to be sung in the home and with the people in the community. You still believe in God, do you?"

"Mother, I read only two pages. If you want to know, it made no sense at all. And I was going to burn it. I really was."

That seemed to make her feel better. But she said I needed to get prayed for. "So God will forgive you," she said.

When I touched the lump on my head I thought what needed doing was kicking Josh-Vetter in the rear end. Boy, I hated him. He was even more stupid than Holden Caulfield. Different belief. Where'd he dream up something like that? Was he crazy?

On Monday morning after chores, I stood behind the shelterbelt for a long time and spied on the shack again. "Girl, it's your fault," I said to the air. "Who leaves books lying around in an old shack, anyway? That's the weirdest thing I have ever heard of. Hey, just leave me alone. I want nothing to do with your stupid books."

At half-to-nine lunch I drank three cups of coffee and ate three slices of cheesetoast. The way I figured, everybody was just plain stupid. Maybe someday when I got to be as old as Jake, I would run away to the world and be a preacher. I would start up my own colony of religious people. I would show them what I could do. I wasn't stupid. I would preach all over the world. Millions of people would become religious because of me.

"Haven't you had enough?" Lisbeth asked when I asked for the fourth piece of cheesetoast.

"Let him eat," my mother said. "He's growing."

"He's growing into a coffee pot," Jake said.

After coffee my mother didn't even give me a chance to lie about having to go to the goosebarn. She clutched my arm with muscles I never knew she had.

"It's high time you earned your lunches around here," she said.

She put me to work helping Jake upholster a bench. He seemed glad to have help. He fumbled with the material, trying to stretch it tight. The sponge stuffing kept escaping as he tried to staple the leatherette to the bottom of the board.

"Here, stretch it tight while I staple," he said. I took hold of the edge and pulled it tight. We worked in silence for a minute.

"So, do you like feeding the geese?" Jake asked.

"I dunno."

Jake lifted his eyebrows. "What do you mean, you don't know?"

"I don't know," I said stubbornly. There'd been a time when I told Jake everything. It'd been just us then. The two Wolner cowboys of Rockyview. He'd shown me how to ride Madeline and throw a loop. Even after he'd gone to work on the fields driving a cultivator, he'd still come to the cowbarn once a week to ride Madeline. But after that winter he worked in the pigbarn with the pigman, he had started changing.

Jake stopped stapling. "Listen, I told Mother I was sorry. Do you think I'd have talked like that if I would've known Mother was listening?"

"You should stay away from that drinker."

"Boy, that's real bright. For your information, Father sent me down there last week because the elders hadn't elected the second pigman yet. Do you have an idea how much work there is in an operation like that? Flat Willow would be nothing if we didn't have the pigs. You ought to stick your nose in there sometime."

"Not as long as that drinker's down there. You know what Father always says. 'Bad companions spoil good customs'."

Jake laughed. "Oh yeah? What about you?" He aimed the stapler at my chest. "The raven shouldn't call the crow black.

What were you doing, reading the Testament together with pocketbooks? Did you sing too? Listen, someone who drinks a little isn't as dangerous as someone with ideas about different beliefs in his head. You know what happens to those people. They're the ones who leave the colony and spread rumours out there in the world."

I stayed quiet. I didn't want to get into that argument. That stupid Josh-Vetter. Thinking I might have a different belief. Boy, he was stupid.

At half-to-ten my father parked his truck in front of our unit. He went from room to room. My sisters scurried in front of him, all talking at once as they showed him the progress they'd made. They were getting ready for the Moon Ranch boys to lay the linoleum. My father filled his thermos at the drinking-water tap, then stopped to watch Jake and me.

"Peter," he said. "Will you come to the field with me?"

I jumped up and Jake waved. "Go, before Mother sees you."

But my mother saw me. "Just make sure he's back in time for dinner, Zack," she said.

As I climbed into the field truck, I felt good. It was always good riding in the truck with my father. He loved the fields. He'd said once that he was the luckiest man alive because God had given him the job he loved.

My father straightened his straw hat and slipped on his dark sunglasses. "Shall we go, then?" he said.

At the intersection near the truck scale and granaries, he turned and drove eastward along a dirt road. The land was straight and level, a patchwork of green and golden strips, alternating with dark summerfallow. Occasionally, a lone clump of poplars drifted by, and here and there shelterbelts stretched across the prairie like straight-edges. My father explained that the previous landowners had planted the Siberian Elm shelterbelts to keep wind erosion down.

"Why do we call it Flat Willow, then?" I asked.

My father smiled. "The area was already named before we came. The landowners had a poor man. They suggested the name because of him. They said he hardly ever said the word "tree". It was always willows. Caragana were willows, elms were willows, everything was willows to him. As if God had made only one kind of tree." He became thoughtful and rubbed his beard. A troubled look came over his face. But he was quiet.

I stared at my chapped black shoes, at the dusty floor of the truck, and then studied my father closely, proud of the way he steered the truck and shifted the gears. I wished he knew how proud I was of him. I stuck my arm out the window and played with the wind for a while.

"Father, did you really want to move here?" I finally asked, searching his face.

"It made no difference," he said. "You have to care and not care at the same time. That's a Gmanshofter's way. Our communities are the arks of the world. The sermon says all those who didn't live in the ark drowned in the flood."

I kept playing with the wind, directing it so it shot into the truck, against my face. The wind was warm and smelled of ripe wheat fields and thistles and diesel smoke.

"Father?"

"Yes?"

I hesitated.

"What were you going to ask me, Peter?"

"Could it be? — and I'm sure there's not a single one — but I'm just wondering about it...could it be that somewhere out there...among the thousands and thousands of people in the world...could it be, that maybe there is one person who has half a chance of getting into heaven?"

My father laughed. "Well, Peter, that was some long and complicated question. Yes, the Bible says the good people will come from all corners of the world."

"Could Alberta — or Saskatchewan, even — be a corner like that?"

My father frowned. "Why do you ask?"

"I'm just wondering."

My father said nothing for a while. I thought he wouldn't answer my question. But he did.

"There are people out there," he said, "who are as good as we are. But because they weren't born in the ark, you can't blame them for not knowing the way. But God will decide. It's not for us to decide."

My father was the smartest man in the whole world. I wished I could tell him that. I wished I could reach over and hug him like I did so many years ago. But I knew better.

My father shifted down the truck. He turned off the road and drove on a rut-road alongside a shelterbelt. Two swathers, one John Deere and one Versatile, drifted into view. I tried counting how often the reels went around per minute. The reels swept the cut wheat stems onto the canvas belts which carried it to the centre and fed it to the ground in a swath. A swather was the funniest-looking machine on the field. It had two wheels in front and one in the back — the opposite of a tricycle. It seemed as if the rear wheel steered the machine, but it didn't.

"In order to turn," my father said, "one of the front wheels stops turning, while the other doesn't. It's like the good and the bad. If it's not the good that's steering you, it's the bad. If you're not going forward with your life, you're most certainly going backwards."

He drove the field truck right up close to the swathers, and they both stopped. The engineer on the John Deere was an old bachelor named Sommel Wipf. He jumped off the swather and stepped over a swath perched on the fresh stubble. He stretched his long legs and jiggled his black pants, then leaned into the truck.

"Did you bring the pulley puller?" he asked. My father nodded. Sommel's face was red from the sun and his shirt-sleeves were rolled almost to his shoulders. He gave the peak of my katus a pull.

"How's the cowboy?" he asked.

I gave him a quizzical look.

"Oh yeah, we got no cows," he laughed, as if he hadn't known. I liked Sommel. People said he was full of good bullshit. He was always joking around. He'd been baptised for many years, but was still beardless because men didn't wear beards until after they got married. But I knew something about old Sommbalitz that he probably didn't realize I knew. Sometimes having older sisters came in handy. When you tuned your ears, you could pick up some interesting facts about people. Sommel never married with anybody because the only girl he ever wanted was his cousin Rachel. Cousins couldn't get married.

"It's a good crop, Zack," he said. "It'll yield forty bushels for sure."

"Praise God," my father said, and Sommel Wipf said, "Yo, for sure."

We got out of the truck and my father walked over to the Versatile swather. The engineer on the Versatile was also named Sommel. He was from the Kleinser clan, and about Jake's age. He wore a green farm cap with the jumping John Deere on it, and he smelled of cigarettes. I noticed, as my father inspected a wobbly pulley at the side of the swather, that Kleinser Sommel kept moving around, always staying downwind from my father.

"I'll fuel the John Deere up first, so that at least one of you can get going right away," my father said.

He walked back to his truck and in a minute he was backed up behind the John Deere swather. Sommel Wipf took the nozzle and hose from where it was attached to the blue fuel tank on the back of the truck. Then my father took the pulley puller from his tool-box and Kleinser Sommel slipped the large V-belt off the bad pulley. My father had shown me once how a pulley puller worked. It had three claws that fit around the pulley, and you slowly turned a hexagon-headed rod in the hub to pull the pulley evenly off the shaft.

As they worked, my father gave Kleinser Sommel a stern

look. "If that field catches fire because of your gol'darn habit...." He shook his head and scowled.

Kleinser Sommel turned his face away from my father and grinned into the breeze. My father was one of the council brethren already, who sat up front near the preachers' desk at church. Young people were expected to respect baptised people, and the council brethren especially.

I stared at Kleinser Sommel's back for about three minutes. A loaded question was banging around inside my head. Should I just come right out and ask him? Hell, he had no respect for my father, laughing behind his back as he did. Why should I care if I offended *him*?

I moved right up close and tapped Sommel's arm. I figured I was safe in my father's shadow.

"What?" Kleinser Sommel said, turning.

"Kleinser Sommel," I said, "what did you do with that gun you stole from the neighbour?"

Boy oh boy! Some people had no sense of humour. Kleinser Sommel grabbed the front of my shirt faster than you could say "brother-of-a-pigman". He lifted me roughly off the ground and flung me down onto the stubble. My katus popped off my head and rolled away.

"Listen, you little runt." His cigarette breath was in my face. "Say one more word about that, and you're gonna be riding home with a bloody nose. And don't think just because your dad's here I wouldn't do it."

My father just shook his head and kept working. He said absolutely nothing to the Kleinser punk. Kleinser Sommel let go my shirt after a minute and left me lying on the stubble. I got up and walked back to the truck to wait, shaking. Why the devil was everybody so touchy about that gun? Couldn't a person say one word about it?

Later, when my father got into his truck, he turned to me before turning on the ignition. He removed his sunglasses so I could see his eyes. He frowned. "Listen, Peter," he said, squeezing my shoulder hard. "I do not want to hear another word out of you about that gun."

"But Father, I just wanted to know — "

"There's nothing to know, Peter." He tightened his grip. "We want to put that rumour to rest already. If the boys say they didn't steal the gun, no amount of accusations will ever make a difference. Do you understand?"

I nodded, wondering if he'd have let Kleinser Sommel beat me up.

On the way back, my father took the long way home, showing me all the Flat Willow land. The uncut wheat and barley stands rolled like waves in an ocean. I imagined a ship. When it came to a summerfallow strip, the ship ploughed through and into the next field. My father pointed at a coyote trotting in the ditch, his tongue long in the heat. As we drove by, he stepped to the side and disappeared into the grain field.

At home, before I got out of the truck, my father reached over and squeezed my shoulder, gently this time. "Come with me more often," he said. "When you're not *busy* with the geese. There's much to learn on the field."

At the dinner table Ronni mentioned gopher-hunting again. "We found good territory in a pasture over at Mr. Clements' farm," he said.

"I'm not interested," I said.

* * * *

It hadn't occurred to me that the English girl might not be there. I nosed around in the shack, lifting up boards and smelling the wood. I loved the smell of old lumber. It reminded me of the old colony, of the cowbarn, and of Olvetter. I stared out the knocked-out window, waiting. She'd be surprised to see me. Her lonely eyes would get big. "Did you finish that classic book?" "No. My uncle Josh burned it." "Why?" "Because." "But why?" "I don't know. Because of all the swear words, I guess. He and my brother Jake and the pigman, they're the most stupid people in the world. They're as stupid as Holden Caulfield. You know what my uncle Josh said?" "What?" "He said I was going over to another religion. He's so stupid."

No way. She wouldn't ask these questions. And I wouldn't tell her about Jake and Josh-Vetter. She wouldn't understand, anyway.

I waited for about an hour, but she didn't come. I decided to walk around the hill behind the shack to peek at her farm. There were actually three hills there, one after another. The girl's farm sat behind the third hill. It was pitifully small. All it had were two weathered quonsets with a rusty auger parked nearby, and a small metal machine shed. There was one small two-storey house, painted smoke gray. A TV antenna stood like a rake from behind the roofpeak. They were the most sorry-looking buildings I had ever seen. At the back, a toothless barbed-wire fence leaned almost to the ground. Her farm wasn't even a shadow of the proud ark of Flat Willow. No wonder she was lonely.

I trudged back to Flat Willow for half-to-three lunch, cursing myself for being so stupid. Why should I care about someone who wasn't in the ark? They weren't even in the right corner of the world, because they had a TV. Televisions were evil. Then my father's words came back to me: "God will decide." I was glad it wasn't up to me.

Lena was cutting a saskatoon berry cheesecake when I walked down the basement stairs. She looked up and smiled, but said nothing. The coffee kettle sang on the cooker. I sat down at the table and watched her. Soon everybody came, and we lunched. Nobody seemed to notice I wasn't saying a word.

Petch's son Christoph pointed to his plate. "Lena, this is the best cheesecake in the world," he said.

My sister blushed. It *was* good cheesecake. I wished I could steal a piece and take it to that lonely English girl. She was probably starving this very minute.

After chores I walked back to the shack again. I didn't feel like drawing. All I could think about was the English girl. I waited in the shack for half an hour. Then, on the road along the coulee, a truck roared. It was probably my father.

"Hi, Peter Waldner."

I jumped. I hadn't seen her walk up. She had come around the side of the shack.

"So, you decided to come back?" she said.

"Yeah."

"Did I scare you?"

"Yeah."

I tried not to stare. She was wearing a light blue and white striped dress and a headband of the same colour. Around her neck hung a silver necklace with a blue-white crystal. And she wore sandals. She didn't seem like the same person I'd met the other day. I must have stared too much.

"What's wrong, Peter Waldner?" she asked, sticking the book in her hand into her pocket.

I shrugged. "Nothing."

The girl said in an excited voice, "Guess what, Peter? Your preacher man came to see us this morning."

"Why?"

"He took the chimes from the boy who stole them and brought them back to us."

"How did he know they belonged to you?"

"This shack is on Uncle Frank's land."

Tessa walked to the rock and hoisted herself up and sat. I wished I had some gum. I smiled when I thought about that. Sara had told me about gum. A boy was supposed to have a packet of gum in his pocket because girls liked to receive gum from boys. When they sang the song "Church In The Wildwood," they sang "Gum gum gum, to the church in the wildwood" at the chorus. A boy with gum in his pocket was a popular fellow. Funny, the other day the English girl had been the one with the gum.

"Do you know anything about the ark?" I asked, sitting down on the doorstep of the shack.

"Noah's ark?"

"Well, yeah...the ark."

She slid off the rock and walked toward me. Her eyes sparkled. "You know what? In the summer, every time it rained, Pierre said he would like to be like Noah. He said when the next flood came, he would ask God for the job of building the ark."

"Did he really say that?"

"Yeah. Pierre was pretty funny sometimes." She sat down beside me.

"Was he really good with the animals?"

"He sure was," she said. "When the men brought the first load of pigs, Uncle Frank couldn't keep Pierre away from there. Pierre seemed right at home in the pigbarn, as if he'd been a pig farmer all his life."

"But could he tame them as people said?"

"Yeah. The fat man there told me and Uncle Frank that Pierre had a special gift. He said sows get fierce when someone takes away their piglets, but when Pierre was around, you could actually reach out and pat them."

"Did *you* see that happen?"

"No. The fat man said so."

"I wouldn't trust the pigman. He drinks a lot of whiskey."

She touched my arm. "I know, but that doesn't mean he lied about Pierre calming the sows."

I shook my head. "I'd believe it if I saw someone look Big Bull at Rockyview in the eye and tame him. There's no fiercer animal than a bull."

"Peter, you don't have to see everything to believe it. Aunt Mae believed it, and she didn't even hear it from the fat man. She said, in spite of Pierre's bad temper, he really might've had an angel with him without knowing it."

"I don't believe that."

"You don't believe in angels?"

"I don't believe they come down any more. They did that only in the Bible."

"Aunt Mae said there are angels everywhere. She told me about a man in Saskatoon who talked with one."

"I don't believe it."

"Why don't you believe it?"

"Because."

The girl stood up and walked back to the rock and lifted herself up on it again.

"It's wrong to believe something that's not in the Bible," I said.

She gave me a challenging look and shook her head. "Peter Waldner, I think you'll be a preacher someday. I just know it. You have preacher written all over you."

I laughed. A lot of people had said I'd be the preacher.

"We're moving to Alberta next week," she said.

"Hey, that's where we came from."

"Maybe you could move back with us," she said, smiling at her fingernails.

"That'd be running away," I said sharply.

There was a moment of silence.

"Do you think you'll stay here forever?" she asked.

"My mother would have a heart attack if I ran away," I said. I thought about asking her if she would ever run away. But then I thought about what a silly question that would be. She was already out in the world. Where would she run to? Unless she ran away to Saudi Arabia.

"Have you ever been to Saudi Arabia?" I asked.

The girl laughed. "Why would I go to Saudi Arabia?"

"Why not?"

"That's thousands of miles away. It takes a lot of money to get there. And it's a different culture. You don't just up and go to Saudi Arabia."

"Oh," I said.

Just then the bell rang at Flat Willow. I tugged my watch from my pants. Supper for the little kids.

"What's it like to live in a Hutterite community, anyway?" Tessa asked.

I shrugged. "It's okay."

"I mean, you're so strange."

I frowned. "Don't say that. There are plenty of rumours about us already."

"Gee, you're touchy, Peter Waldner," she said. "I'm sorry I said *strange*. I meant *different*."

"That's the way people are supposed to be," I said.

"Peter, I remember the first time I saw Hutterites, in Swift Current. I was only six years old. I asked my mother if the men belonged to a gang of black cowboys. They had on their big black hats and black suits. Please don't get mad at me for asking, but why do they dress like cowboys?"

I laughed. Jake would laugh too. Gang of cowboys. The Communal Cowboy Gang. Or the Black Cowboy Gang. Jake liked those kinds of sayings. We could be in westerns. The more I thought about that, the funnier it seemed.

"What's so funny?"

"I bet if you put some of the boys on a horse, they would slide right off," I said. "The horse wouldn't even have to move an inch, and they'd tumble off. Just because someone looks like a cowboy doesn't automatically make him a cowboy. You have to know about horses and cattle and about milking cows and riding in the foothills."

"Are you a cowboy, then?"

"I was the cowboy at the old colony."

Tessa made big eyes. "Hey, that's neat," she said. "I'm talking to a real cowboy. And I bet you were a good one too."

I shrugged again. "Oh well."

"Is that why you draw westerns?"

"Sort of. But I was an artist long before I became the cowboy."

The girl slid off the rock again. "Pierre was a cowboy before he was nine years old."

"Really?"

"Yeah, Aunt Mae gave us pictures of him when he was a kid. And he had a horse too."

"What happened? Did he have to move away too?"

She shook her head sadly. "Pierre didn't remember much. He had amnesia about certain things. Especially about before he was nine years old."

"How do you know he was a cowboy, then?"

"From the pictures."

"Oh."

The girl sat down beside me again on the doorstep and stared at the ground. When she looked up, she tugged at my arm.

"Peter, have you ever wanted something so badly, you pretended you had it?"

I thought for a minute. In a way, I'd always had what I really wanted. I'd wanted to be the cowboy, and Dan-Vetter had asked me to be his helper. I wasn't sure if day-dreaming in church about riding in the foothills or flying around the world in a supersonic jet with Hufer Maria was really pretending. Those were just thoughts. And they never were more than just that.

"My cousin Mike Hofer and me, well, we sort of pretended we were sheriffs, and we rode Madeline in the foothills near the Rocky Mountains and chased outlaws."

She smiled. "It was kinda silly, but when Pierre came to live with us, I pretended he was my real brother. I always wanted to have a brother. Pierre was old enough to be my dad, but I didn't care. With his mind being slow and all, he was perfect for a brother. Pierre loved it here. The treatments he'd had, had worked, and we thought we'd have him for a long time. He was so much at home out here."

I looked at her face as she talked, and I felt like touching her hand. But I didn't.

She continued. "But even then, my dad — Aunt Mae said he was too superstitious — said it wasn't a good idea to have him live with us. He thought Pierre might be like Lennie in the book called *Of Mice and Men*. Pierre was big like Lennie, and he loved animals just like Lennie did. Peter, you should read that book. It's a classic. But in the book, Lennie always tried keeping mice for pets, only he would pet them too much, and they'd die. And Dad was afraid Pierre would hug me too much one day and break my neck just like Lennie broke the woman's neck in that book. Aunt Mae told Dad he was crazy. 'The book is just fiction,' she said. But that's how my dad used to be. He always thought about the worst things...."

Suddenly I slipped into a memory from Rockyview. I was standing beside a pile of seed potatoes at the bottom of a dark rootcellar. The musty odour of old potatoes and burlap sacks was in my nose. It was cool and dim, and I was alone. For some reason, the German teacher wasn't there. Then I remembered. I was six years old. It was my first day out of kindergarten, and I was a gardenboy. I was the oldest of all the kids in my year. The older gardenboys were in English school. I was playing with a potato when suddenly it got darker in the rootcellar. I turned. A big man stood in the doorway. He came toward me. He took jerky steps, and his arms were in front of him. He was trying to speak to me, but all he did was moan and sputter. Then he was right under the bulb. He had a flat forehead and his piercing eyes were deep-set, and they looked in two directions. I shrank against the pile of seed potatoes. The man came closer. His arms reached toward me and he kept mumbling and moaning. He had very crooked teeth, and a bubble of saliva hung from his mouth. I screamed, and picked up a potato and threw it at him. Then, screaming and crying, I ran to the top part of the rootcellar. That's where I ran into the chickenman and an English woman. The English woman was an egg customer, and her car was parked at the chickenbarn nearby. She ran down into the rootcellar after her mumbling man.

"Did I spook you again?" The girl tugged at my arm. "You seem spooked."

I nodded.

"Why do you spook so easily?" she said. "Did someone hurt you?"

I said nothing. I wasn't sure what she meant. Josh-Vetter had hurt me when he rapped my head with the screwdriver. My father and the German teacher had strapped me a few times, but that was nothing. Getting hit over the head with a screwdriver — *that* was different.

Tessa leaned in front of me. "Do you have bad memories? Aunt Mae says sometimes people have bad memories from when they were little kids."

I looked at her eyes for a minute. There was warmth in there, and she seemed so wise.

"Do you promise not to laugh if I tell you, Tessa?" It was the first time I'd said her name.

She said softly, "Of course not, Peter Waldner."

I told her about the rootcellar. As I told it, she held my arm as if she was a nurse and I was her patient. She nodded a lot.

"Well, Peter Waldner," she said when I was finished, "I can assure you, you wouldn't have been afraid of Pierre. Sure, he got angry sometimes, but he was great to have around."

"Why did he get angry?"

She shrugged. "Doesn't everybody get angry once in a while?"

I straightened myself on the doorstep. "Why did he walk out in that storm, anyway?" I asked. "Was he angry at someone? Didn't he know there was a blizzard?"

She cast her gaze to the ground very quickly. "You'd have to ask him," she said. "Nobody knows."

I wanted to ask her if she knew anything about the stolen gun, but decided not to. When she said "nobody knows" the sad look came back to her eyes. I knew she didn't want to talk about the man's death. Maybe it was best to forget about it, and, as my father had said, let it rest. Why should it matter to me, anyway?

Chapter Nine

Before the linoleum covered it up, the plywood floor was a mess. It had dried paint spots all over and some turpentine clouds where my sisters had accidentally spilled a little paint. The Moon Ranch boys and Jake got on their knees and filled the knot-holes with wood filler. Then they sanded and vacuumed the floor. Jake showed me how to hold the wide putty knife, and I helped them spread the linoleum glue on the floor. It looked like stringy mud and had a mild smell, like two-day-old varnish or something.

I joked with Jake and the Moon Ranch boys and said we should call ourselves the Linoleum Gang. They gave me confused looks at first, but Jake caught on and suggested we call ourselves The Linoleum Cowboys. I knew he was trying to schmier himself over to my side again and make things right after what had happened on Friday. I let him. Heck, boozer or not, he was the only brother I had. Tessa had none.

After we rolled out the linoleum, the room looked instantly finished. And it seemed brighter now. Bigger. The linoleum design was sort of weird, though. It looked like gray and white confetti that had been dumped on the floor and flattened out evenly. My sisters, planning ahead, excitedly held various curtain fabric samples over the window edges and against the linoleum.

I thought about Tessa all evening. Boy, would my sisters have something to tease me about now! If I went back there, I'd have to watch for the gardenboys, because if they knew I wasn't going to that shack merely because I liked old buildings, they would blabber it over the whole world. I wished Tessa could see us roll out the linoleum, though. And I wished she could see the houses. I knew she'd like my sisters. Especially Sara. "She's smart like you, Tessa," I would say. "Mind you, she's fifteen already. She's nosey, though — wants to know everything. But I'm not telling her anything. She'd tell, and my father would tell me I should stay away from the shack. My mother would have a heart attack. Last evening we laid most of the linoleum. David, that's one of our helpers from Moon Ranch, gave me the job of rolling the press. It took out the bubbles and made the glue stick tight. Boy, that press was heavy." "How heavy, Peter?" "I don't know. Heavy...damn heavy." "Peter, you said a swear word." "I don't care. If my uncle Josh can swear, I can too." Geez, my uncle was stupid. "Josh-Vetter, you mind your own business, you smoker. You're not my father, okay? Just leave me alone, you hypocrite. You are so cottonpicken' stupid, Josh-Vetter. Different belief! Are you sure you don't have a screw loose or something?"

Later, at half-to-ten lunch in the basement, my mother announced that Petch was coming on Wednesday to fetch his sons back to Moon Ranch. We pretty much had the work under control, and they could finish laying all the linoleum by then. She said the boys could quit early that evening.

Jake and Christoph stood up at the same time. Christoph had a sly look on his face. "Well, in that case, I'm gonna shower up," he said, giving his suspenders a flick.

Lisbeth rocked back and forth. "Hmmmmmm. I bet I know what their plans are," she said. "And I bet I know who the girls are."

They just grinned, and hurried off.

Sara whispered into my ear and told me what was going on. She always told me things like that, as if I needed to know. Jake and Christoph had their eyes on some girls at Dorothea's unit. Dorothea had two girl helpers from the Kleinser clan's relatives at Old Lakeville colony by Moose Jaw, and Christoph had already asked one of them to be his girlfriend.

"Jake, is it serious already with you too?" Lisbeth called after them. Jake didn't answer. That Lisbeth. She read Harlequin romance books, and thought about romance a lot. I knew what I was in for once I turned fourteen and became a member of the grownups. She'd been trying to couple Jake with every girl who wasn't a cousin for a long time.

Then Olvetter came along. Lisbeth quickly set a chair for him and offered him coffee.

"No, I wouldn't be able to sleep," he said.

"But you *will* have a piece of rhubarb pie, Olvetter, won't you?" Lena said. "I made it."

He took that. But then he needed something to drink with it and asked for coffee anyway, made weak with lots of cream.

When Olvetter singled someone out, you knew ahead of time who it was. He'd fix his steadfast eyes on you and sort of fasten them to you like a trailer to a drawbar hitch or something. From the way he stared at me, I knew I was marked down for something. He'd been thinking about me — not Jake, not my sisters, not my parents, but me, the gooseboy. And he seemed to eat the rhubarb pie with great haste, washing it down with his cream-coffee. Even as he clasped his hands to pray after eating, one of his legs was away from the table already.

"Come with me, Peter," he said.

"Why, Olvetter? It's late already."

"Nein, mein knabe," he said. "It's never too late. Komm doch mit mir, Petrus."

My heart gave a leap. When Olvetter started talking in Bible German, calling me Petrus like Apostle Peter was called in the Bible, I knew it was serious. Religiously serious.

I followed him to his temporary unit.

"Petrus," he said, as he hung his black hat on his hat rack, "I have something to tell you."

Lord, I could see it coming. A sermon about the end of the world. Didn't he know that I'd already *tried* being extremely religious on Sunday? Didn't he know that I was happy the way I was? Today, after the long ride in the truck with my father, then talking to Tessa again, laying linoleum with Jake and the Moon Ranch boys, I'd started thinking Flat Willow was a swell place, after all. Why make it complicated again?

"Sitz nieder." Olvetter motioned toward a chair at the table, and switched on the table lamp. He walked to his bookshelf and took down one of his heavy black volumes.

"Peter, I want you to start reading the Chronicles," he said, setting the book down on the table, then sitting down on the chair beside mine. The book was about two inches thick and had golden letters on the cover.

"But Olvetter, I can't read that by myself yet. It's too hard to read. The German isn't like Bible German. It's difficult."

He picked his round reading glasses off the table and slipped them on. "Not to worry, Peter," he said. "We now have our Chronicles in English."

He opened the big book. It smelled of fresh ink and glue. He placed his finger on the imprints on the title page. Sure enough, it was in English. It was called *The Chronicles of the Hutterian Brethren, Volume I.*

"See. The good Gmanshofter down in New York translated it for us," he said. His eyes gleamed, and seemed hopeful.

He flipped a few pages. "In Austria and Moravia the forebears spoke German. Then, when they moved to Russia, they learned how to speak Russian too. Well, we've been here over a hundred years where people speak English. With the good English teachers we have these days, the young people speak English better than German already. God doesn't care what language we speak, as long as we speak *His* language. We can thank God for those good people down in New York. So now,

Peter, you have no excuse for not reading the Chronicles if you need to interest yourself with something."

"But Olvetter, I can't take *your* book. What would you read?"

"Have no angst, your father will be getting one through the post too," he said.

I sighed with relief and nodded quickly. "Okay. So when it comes, then I'll start reading. I'll start right at page one and read all the way through. You can believe that."

Olvetter looked over the top of his reading glasses. He shook his head. "But until it arrives, you can come and read from my copy in the evenings when you're not busy with the geese."

I stared at the pages. Olvetter could sure make it difficult. It wasn't that I didn't already know some of what the Chronicles were about. My father had read out loud from the Chronicles called *Das Grose Geshichtbuch Der Hutterischen Brüder* every Saturday on winter evenings since I could remember. Saturday evenings were the Holy Evenings, when people sang the forebears' songs with even greater fervour than on regular evenings. On Saturday evenings we didn't need to memorize the German verses of those songs for recital in German school next morning, because there was no German school on Sunday mornings. Those evenings were free from school troubles, yet they weren't entirely free. Reading the Chronicles was a duty every Gmanshofter owed to the forebears.

But they were tough to read, and made you think serious thoughts. Deep thoughts. Many people didn't read the Chronicles any more. Maybe they were lazy, maybe there were too many material things to think about. The Chronicles told about the forbears' struggles in the Old Country, in places like Austria, Moravia and Russia. They were mostly about tough times, about persecution. Many people got killed for their beliefs. In those days, people who didn't believe in the Catholics and in the wars got their heads chopped off, were burned alive at the stake, or left to rot in dark dungeons. The Chronicles told about the forebears fleeing from one country to another, always fleeing from wars, from the Turks and from the Catholics. When you read them, you felt like a sinner all over again, a pale light compared to the forebears. You could never hope to be as pious as they had been.

"You must know," Olvetter was talking, "our people have had peace for a long time already. And now people live as if peace will last forever. But what if the war came again? And what if the government changes the rules again and tries to pull us into the war? And then? Will we have the strength the forebears had? What happens when a grain of wheat falls from the head? Can you expect it to grow back?"

"I suppose not," I said.

"Right. When a grain of wheat falls, it must die before it can rise again. It must die to God's plan. If its destiny is bread, it must get broken up and mixed together and become one with its companions in the dough. Then, it can rise again and give nourishment. Likewise, if its destiny is to grow again, it must first suffer death in the ground, and only then can it put forth roots, and spring forth anew."

"Olvetter, I promise, when the winter comes I'll read the entire book all the way through," I said. "I might even read it twice."

Olvetter took a deep breath and shook his head. "Petrus, now, don't look to the floor. Look on my face. That's better. Now tell me — and you know the story too. What happened to five of those ten brides, the unwise ones, who took their lamps to meet the groom, but failed to fill them with oil?"

I shrugged. "I guess they weren't let into heaven."

"Now, Petrus." He laid his hand on my shoulder. "What good can come out of reading pocketbooks? Is that putting oil in your lamp?"

I stared at the floor.

"You don't know?"

"I didn't read that book. I saw what kind of book it was, so I didn't read it."

"Who gave it to you?"

"I found it."

"Where?"

I could lie without blinking to my father, my mother — anyone. But not to Olvetter. Lying to him was like lying to the forebears.

"I found it in that old shack," I said.

The old man straightened himself in his chair. "I risk filling your head with pride when I tell you that you are a smart boy," he said. "It's good to be smart. It's God's gift. But sometimes the smart ones are the worst off because their cleverness swells up their heads, and they become the most stupid. Our foundation is built on what the forebears struggled for. You must build a basis on which to rest the things you learn. Otherwise you'll get blown away like chaff out the back of a combine. Do you understand?"

"Yes." I wasn't sure I understood it all, but I hoped that, deep down, a part of me did.

Olvetter squeezed my shoulder and stood up. "Go now. I'm going to bed."

I sat outside on the steps for a long time, listening to my parents sing. In the unit next to ours, the blacksmith and his family sang the same song. There were six girls in that family, and they all sang in the evenings. I thought that if I ever got married, I might pick one of Shmied Sommel's girls. She would know all the melodies. I followed the words, but I didn't sing along. I knew the words by heart from recital in German school.

Das gewissen shläft im leben
Doch im tode wacht es auf
Da sieht man vor augen shweben
Seinen ganzen lebenslauf

Alle seine kostbarkeit
Gäbe man zur selben zeit
Wenn man nur gesheh'ne sachen
Ungeshehen könnte machen

Conscience, it sleeps in life
Yet in death from slumber it rises
There, it hovers before the eyes as
Your entire course of life
All earthly wealth, substance won
You'd offer then, and pray
If only ills done in your day
Could yet be caused undone

The night hung over Flat Willow and the world, and out west behind the shelterbelt, over Tessa's poor farm, silent lightning danced in the sky. Although it was a warm night, I shivered with the lightning.

Chapter Ten

I always saw the span of a week like the path the sun makes across the sky. Wednesday stood on top. Funny how you remember some days of the week, though. Wednesday was gashtel suppen day, my favourite soup. I had loved those crumb dumplings with duck for dinner since I was old enough to remember having eaten them. But the soup had nothing to do with that Wednesday in August at Flat Willow. And it wasn't the juicy duck, either, because the duck supply in the locker always ran out in May, and after that we ate chickens with the gashtel suppen until duck-slaughtering time. Today, it was the sun. The *hot* sun. It climbed to mid-heaven, and seemed to park there for a while, the blistering light laying bare the whole world. The ducks and geese were too lazy to eat, but crowded around the water troughs, dipping their beaks often and quickly, then pointing to the sun like the bulrushes down by the slough. The day crawled too — till the watermelons came. Anna and Judy gushed into the house with the news. An English woman with a white refrigerator-type truck had parked by the kuchel.

My father was combing his beard at the mirror in the hallway. He was going to Swift Current for combine parts. "Now there's a smart woman," he said.

My mother and I edged down the basement stairs, carrying a laundry basket loaded with jars of canned fruit left over from all the lunching in the last two weeks.

"Ha!" she said.

"Can I go?" I asked, as we carried the basket through the

corridor that led to the coldroom. My mother said nothing, which I took to mean yes.

A crowd of excited girls and women had already gathered at the truck. It was easy to pick out the English woman. In the cluster of people wearing long colourful skirts and black and white kerchiefs, she was the only one wearing blue jeans and a white T-shirt. But as I drew closer, I saw there were two English people there. Beside the woman, with her hands in her back pockets, stood Tessa. What in heaven was she doing along with the fruit truck? I made a wide circle and slunk into the crowd from the back. There was a likeness in the two English faces, and I thought they might be sisters. The woman's face and arms were tanned dark. She looked like an Indian already. Her hair was butterscotch-coloured like Tessa's, but very short. Her T-shirt had "University of Regina" on it. She had opened the double-swing doors at the back of her truck, and as people pressed close to see, they said, "Ohhhh, a truckload of gietsch."

"What gives here?" The hauswirt shoved through the crowd. The women, standing with their arms crossed as if posing for a picture, hinted loudly about how good the watermelons would be.

"Have patience, we will look," he said. He took his straw hat off and dabbed at his hair and forehead with a red handkerchief. When he saw the watermelons, he gave an approving nod, and the hesitant look on his face melted into a wide smile. The entire floor of the truck was covered with watermelons, and cool sweet-smelling air wafted over our heads.

"You're a timely salesman," the hauswirt said to the woman, but then he quickly said, "I mean *saleswoman*."

The woman looked at Tessa and they both smiled.

Then the preacher arrived. The elders talked with the woman for a few minutes, then stepped to the side. They motioned to Olvetter and Speed Jahannes-Vetter, who had just walked up, to follow them. Speed Jahannes-Vetter walked very slowly.

Tessa smiled meekly at the staring school girls at the front of the crowd. Someone pushed a kindergarten kid, who inched up curiously to Tessa and touched her hand as if it were red hot. The school girls looked at each other and giggled.

I caught a whiff of pig smell suddenly and Chuck the pigman wheezed past me.

"That's the neighbour's kid," he said. Beside him stood my sister's man Kleinser Thom. The elders had elected Thom to be the second pigman of Flat Willow. "She's the one who used to come across the coulee with that poor man to see the pigs before the problems started," the fat brother said.

I stared at the pigman. What the devil was he talking about? What problems? I was about to nudge Thom and ask him, when the preacher appeared from behind the truck, and waved them over for council. As they followed the preacher, I thought about how different those two were. They weren't just baptised brothers of the community, they were brothers like Jake and I were brothers. But the big difference was in how they looked. Chuck was a big-bellied barrel, while Thom was just a post. I had nothing against the thin one. He was okay in my book. But the fat one — he'd made himself plenty of enemies with his dealings. "One wolf knows another," people always said. At Rockyview he'd latch onto the worst kind of sinners when he went to Lethbridge. The kind who hung out in the bars and smoked like steamers. He'd even been caught in an evil place once, where women go up on a stage and pull their clothes off. Gmanshofter easily forgave one another for their trespasses. At least our daily prayer said we did. But *forgetting* some of the things the pigman had done — that was a different story. He was evil. No two ways about it. *I* knew he was evil because of that stunt he'd pulled on me, telling me my mother had died. Then there was the time when I was nine years old. Some boys and I had gone into the pigbarn. He walked up behind us, grabbed me around the waist and carried me into the breeder barn. And he held me over the pen of a vicious black boar. The boar grunted and spit his slop in my face. His snout, ready to tear my head off, was just inches away. Hell, I almost died from fright there. And my katus fell off and rolled down the pen and stopped at the slats, on a patch of wet, stinking pig manure. He was a devil, all right. His mind was loaded with weeds. I figured he was getting a free ride on the ark.

I slunk around the side of the truck and spied on the men discussing the deal. They'd asked the English woman and the hauswirt's wife to join their meeting. Wipf Sanna-Pasel, the hauswirt's wife, was counting on her fingers.

"We'll buy the whole truckload if you give us that price," the hauswirt was saying.

"But I normally make a better profit — "

The hauswirt touched the woman's arm. "But neither do you sell a whole truckload of watermelons at one stop. Listen, Miss Longman, in the time it would take you to sell that load of watermelons, you could be halfway to British Columbia for that load of peaches. You see, we're not your average roadside deal."

"But can I be assured our agreed price for the peaches will stick, Mr. Wipf?" she asked.

"If they're as good as you say they are, we'll buy 'em," the hauswirt said.

"Okay, it's a deal then." The woman shook the hauswirt's hand.

She climbed onto the back of the truck and took Tessa's hand to help her climb up too. The hauswirt joined them, and the three passed watermelons to the girls on the ground. Wipf Sanna-Pasel took charge then. She was the boss over the women when there was communal work. She called out orders, and the women organized a long line of watermelons in individual piles on the gravel road beside the kuchel. There were two watermelons for every soul in the community.

Soon other women and girls arrived with laundry wagons to haul the watermelons away.

Lisbeth tugged at my arm. "Peter, help me load ours."

Tessa spotted me as we loaded the wagon for the second time. The truck was empty by then. She waved, jumped off the truck, and started toward us. Oh Lord, what now? *No, Tessa. Don't say anything. These are my sisters here. You don't know Lisbeth. She's the biggest teaser in the whole world.*

I shifted aside and, pretending I hadn't seen her, piled watermelons frantically. A big one slipped from my fingers. It fell to the ground and started rolling.

"Be careful, Peter," Lisbeth called out. "Don't crack them."

I started after the watermelon. The ground was packed smooth and it kept rolling. Someone with blue jeans and white sneakers stepped in front of it. I straightened my back and looked up. Lord, I could already hear my sisters. The whole colony would know. Anna and Judy stared with big eyes, looking Tessa over from head to foot.

"What are you waiting for?" Lisbeth said in German. "She won't bite you. Bring it here, Peter."

I didn't have to. Tessa picked up the watermelon and carried it to the wagon for me.

"Thank you, girl," Lisbeth said, wiping the dust off the watermelon with her apron. She smiled at Tessa. "My brother is a shy one," she said. "But he's cute."

"I know," Tessa said with a giggle, and I wondered what she meant: shy or cute. She grinned slyly at me and I smiled as nonchalantly as I could, though my heart was pounding like a hammermill or something. Lisbeth sure knew how to embarrass you. Still, I knew my secret was safe. Somehow Tessa understood how it was between Gmanshofter and English people. Heck, I could have gone right to her farm and watched television and listened to radio, and I'd still be safe. At that moment I could've given her a squeeze.

Then Lisbeth nudged me. "She really likes you, Peter," she said in German. "Too bad she's an English girl."

Gracious, Lisbeth. Where are your manners? It's not fair. For all this girl knows, you could be saying something awful about her.

"What's your name, girl?" Lisbeth asked.

"Tessa Longman."

"Would you like to see our new houses?" Lisbeth said. "These two girls here would like to show them to you."

"Sure," Tessa said.

"Let's go," Anna said, taking Tessa's arm.

The three girls ran off in front of Lisbeth and me. I pushed the wagon and Lisbeth watched the watermelons to make sure none rolled off. We had piled too many on the wagon.

"She's pretty," Lisbeth said.

I just shrugged and concentrated on pushing the wagon. I wasn't blind.

At home, as Lisbeth and I carried the watermelons down to the basement, Anna and Judy showed Tessa every room in the house. They even ran across to Olvetter's half-unit, which was attached to ours. The Moon Ranch boys were glueing on the baseboards. The girls must have looked into every closet and every corner. Tessa couldn't believe her eyes at all the space. She kept saying, "You have so much room here. It's almost like a mansion." I thought about her sad-looking farm out there. Some things weren't fair. Why couldn't she have been born in the ark like us? Couldn't God have done something to make that happen?

When my mother came along with a laundry basket filled with boxes of crackers and store-bought cookies, she looked suspiciously at Tessa. "What's the English girl doing here?" She spoke German.

"We invited her. She's Peter's girlfriend," Lisbeth said, and I almost died on the spot. She said the word "girlfriend" in English. Anna and Judy burst into giggles.

"Och, Lisbeth!" my mother scolded. "Don't say something like that."

"Mother, I'm just having fun." Lisbeth spoke in English then. "She's such a sweet girl."

She put her arm around Tessa and hugged her, stroking her flowing butterscotch hair. "Look at those nice red cheeks and that beautiful hair. Isn't she a dear?" she said.

That was our Lisbeth, all right. She liked people instantly, and wasn't afraid to show it. Tessa was red in the face, but she smiled. She was a good sport. Boy, I liked that girl.

I ran up the stairs for more watermelons, leaving my sisters to show Tessa more of the house. I wanted to yell out with glee. Nothing was going to stop me from going back to the shack. Maybe later in the day, if I managed to get away from the work. "What'd you think of our houses?" I'd ask. "Did you see my bedroom, Tessa? Pretty big, huh? Me and Jake are sharing it. Did you like my sisters? That Lisbeth, though. She's a teaser. She teases everybody. Especially me. But I'm getting used to it. I wish you could've met Sara. She and Lena were helping over at my sister Dorothea's house. One of these days Dorothea is going to have her first baby."

As I opened the door I thought about how soft I had become since coming to Flat Willow. Why, since Sunday I hadn't even thought much about the cows and Madeline at Rockyview, or about The Cowboy Kid. Instead, here I was, all excited about a girl, and an English girl to boot, about my sisters and houses and Dorothea's baby that wasn't even born yet. Lord, I'd about turned into a regular housecat.

And then I walked into the barrel of a gun.

I jerked back so abruptly that I slipped on the rug and fell backward on my rear. Ronni Kleinser was at the door, pointing a rifle at my head. Behind him stood the gardenboys, chomping watermelon.

"Stick 'em up," Ronni said in an imitation western voice.

What the hell, Ronni? Are you crazy?

"I'm gonna shoot you dead, Wolner Peter."

"RONNI!" I yelled, and I pushed my head down against the rug. I didn't believe Ronni would do it, but if it was loaded, it might go off by mistake.

When I looked up, the boys were laughing, and choking on their watermelon.

"That's for being such a smart aleck, Wolner Peter," Ronni said.

I sat up then. "Is it real?" I asked.

"Yes, but it's kaput." He laid the gun on my legs.

Still shaking, I ran my hand over the barrel, then the stock. I'd never touched a real gun. This one was old. The metal was a dull yellow-gray colour, and pitted with rust. The stock was crinkly, half rotten.

"Where'd you find it?" I said.

"In the slough. We were hot, so we thought we'd go for a swim. But it's so full of crap, you can't swim in there. I saw the barrel sticking out of the water."

"No, you didn't," Jerg Wipf spoke up. "I saw it and I pulled it out."

"Jeepers, imagine it, finding a gun in that slough," I said.

"PETER. ARE YOU CRAZY?"

Lisbeth had come up behind me. She was white in the face. "What are you doing with that gun?" she shouted. "You'll shoot someone."

"It's kaput," I said. "Jerg Wipf pulled it out of the slough in the coulee. See, it's kaput." I felt like teasing Lisbeth a little and pointing it at her head, but I didn't. I was a sinner, but I would never point a rifle at my sister.

Then Tessa huffed up with Anna and Judy. Tessa quickly stepped forward and knelt down beside me. I almost choked. Lord, she smelled of perfume. My sisters must've sprayed a whole glassful on her.

Her eyes were big. "Who pulled it out of the water, Peter?" she said in a low voice.

"What's wrong?"

"It's Mr. Clements' gun — "

"Well, it's mine now." Ronni Kleinser bent down and grabbed it from my knees. "I found it."

At that moment the tanned watermelon woman came around the corner of the unithouse. Beside her walked the preacher and the hauswirt.

"There's that cousin of mine," the watermelon woman said.

Ronni shoved the gun behind his back. But he wasn't quick enough.

"Hold it, hold it. What have we here now?" the preacher said, rushing forward.

Chapter Eleven

As a little school boy, I had grübled over why tractors didn't travel down the road as fast as trucks did. Surely, the huge and powerful 1175 Case that could pull buildings and stoneboats and cultivators ought to have been able to go as fast as the little Mercury pickup. Was it because the drivers forgot to throttle the tractors up when they got to the road? I'd also wondered why adults seldom ran. Even if they were in a hurry, they didn't run. They'd walk in an exaggerated way, their arms pumping like mad. But when the preacher said, "Hold it, hold it," he ran like a young man, his body leaning into the wind. In the swish of a cow's tail he was at Ronni's side and had snatched the gun away. He shoved the barrel against the ground at arm's length and held it there.

"Where did you find this?" The words came out in one breath.

Ronni pointed at Jerg Wipf. "It was him, Olvetter. He found it in the slough."

Kleinser Isaac turned to the chickenman's son, then. He took hold of Jerg's ear, and gave it a tweak that made me wonder if it would stay on his head. Jerg stood on his toes, contorting his body and face in agony.

"Have I not told you to bring things like that to me?" the preacher said in a low, commanding voice.

Jerg bellowed like a calf. Almighty God, he bellowed! There, in front of the English people, he wailed without shame.

I knew the poor guy's ear would be screaming with pain and heat. I'd had my ear twisted like that too. Getting an ear tweaked hurt like hell. But from that day on I understood something about the preacher. He carried two weights in his pocket: one for his family, and one for the others. No wonder some of the bad apples from the Kleinser clan landed so close to the tree.

The preacher gave a quick nod to the hauswirt, and the two elders walked away. Neither of them said a word at first. But once they were out of earshot, they started talking and waving at a great speed.

The English woman tugged at Tessa's sleeve. "Well, Avon Lady, let's vamoose," she said.

"Wouldn't you want coffee and cottage cheese pie first?" Lisbeth asked. "It's almost coffee time."

"Thanks so much, but we have to go."

"How about a tour of our houses then?"

"Thank you so much, but we really need to be going." The woman interlocked her fingers and wriggled her hands. "Maybe next time, though."

My sisters and I, and the gardenboys too, walked back to the truck with the two English people. Resentment sprang up in me. Everything had gone wrong. Everything had happened too fast. Anna and Judy hung close to Tessa as if they owned her, talking as if they'd known her forever. And the gardenboys were beside them, pressing too close, staring too much. I lagged behind, silent, and stubborn.

At the truck, while the two clicked on their seat belts, Lisbeth leaned into the cab. She begged the woman to turn on the radio. "See if Randy Travis is singing," she said. The woman hesitated at first, but then she switched it on — real loud. Right away Lisbeth picked up a song she liked.

"Oh, that's a good one, Holly," she said. "You have no idea how much I love Reba McEntire."

The woman just grinned. Lisbeth swayed with the music

and tapped her foot on the ground. Lord, it was loud! I felt like tapping my foot a little too. The guitar and fiddle music floated out of the truck's dashboard as clear as air and made me feel a little like when Hufer Miechel and I had a contest once to see who could spill out the longest string of swear words without stopping. Dorothea's man Thom had played guitar before he got baptised. We'd listened to him imitate singers called Merle Haggard and Stompin' Tom. But when he got baptised, he had to give all that up. Maybe someday when I'd have forbidden money, I would buy a guitar too. I wished Tessa could be around then to hear me play.

Boy, that music was loud now. The woman had turned it up even louder. I wished I was somewhere else.

Anna nudged me. "It's the schoolteacher," she whispered loudly.

The German teacher was hurrying across the yard, and suddenly we acted as if we'd just stood up from the dead. But Lisbeth didn't care. She had no respect. She wasn't a school girl, and not under the teacher's eye any more. She kept swinging her shoulders to the music and tapping her foot. But then the preacher, scowling like God, appeared from behind the washhouse. Lisbeth stopped dancing and pretended she'd just stood up from the dead also. The watermelon woman clenched her teeth and quickly started up the truck. Tessa waved. I hoped the wave was meant especially for me. Then the truck spun a little gravel and the two drove off in a cloud of dust. The preacher gave Lisbeth a long stare.

"I do not want to see that again," he said, shaking his finger at her. I figured if our Dorothea wasn't married into the Kleinser clan, or if Lisbeth had been one of the Wipfs, there would've been a lot more trouble.

After coffee and chores, I walked across the coulee. The gardenboys were nowhere in sight. On the way, I stopped at the slough. Insects swerved on the placid surface and bubbles rose up though the plankton, and spindly blue dragonflies soared about, now and then kissing the water with feather-like swoops. I skipped a few flat stones. The ripples slowly moved toward the edge, upsetting the blue bowl of sky in the water. How the devil had that gun got in there? Why had Tessa said it was Mr. Clements' gun? Did it have anything to do with the trouble in the pigbarns? Had something happened that the adults didn't tell us about?

Tessa wasn't at the shack. I'd only half expected that she would be. After all, she didn't live in it. I stared blankly at the wall for a while, then decided to walk around the three hills to look at her farm again.

Except for a gray cat sauntering across the yard, the place seemed deserted. Emptiness echoed in me like the call of a loon I'd heard once. What if she had gone to British Columbia with her cousin? What if I never saw her again? What if something happened that made it impossible for either of us to come back to the shack?

On the way home, as I walked past the pigbarn office, my sister's man Thom popped his head out the door.

"Peter, when are you coming in?" he called out, and I jumped. My mind had been travelling again. I hesitated. What if I ran into the fat one?

"Come on, Peter. Your brother told me you haven't looked in here yet. What ails?"

I shrugged sheepishly. Jake had probably told Thom what I'd said on Monday.

"Hey now," he said as I walked up. "*Our* relatives are always welcome in here."

There were three barns, all connected by a central wing. I had seen pictures that someone had snapped from a plane. From the sky, the barns looked like two H's pushed together. Thom showed me the weener hog section first. The metal pens, filled with what seemed like millions of pigs that grunted, squealed, sniffed and stank, stretched so far in front of us that I couldn't see the end. Above the central walkway, on the white plywood ceiling, the bulbs got smaller and smaller till they were just a thin line.

The feeder barn was the same. And as we walked along the walkway, the hogs got bigger, closer to market.

"Flat Willow can pat itself on the back for this operation," Thom said. "It's the best, the newest, the most efficient." He laid his hand on my shoulder. "We're into pigs very, very big" — as if I couldn't see it — "Rockyview has nothing like this. It's a dirt-poor farm. Don't ever kid yourself. We've got the better farm. Sure, they have cows and we don't. But cows...och...cows are nothing. But pigs, boy, you gotta love pigs. They bring in the bacon." He laughed.

I didn't say anything. I still preferred cows.

We walked into the farrow barn. The sows' snouts flew up against the top bars of their crates. They grunted and scolded us for intruding on their litters. I wanted to ask Thom if he had seen Pierre tame the sows, but he talked about pigs nonstop. He'd spent all day castrating piglets, and tomorrow his brother was going to start training him with the breeding program. He talked about different kinds of pigs. I'd had no idea there were that many different breeds. He mentioned Yorkshire, Hampshire, Berkshire, Chester White, Landrace, Duroc — he knew them all. I hoped my sister was extremely proud of him.

"A good pigman is a big asset to a colony these days," Thom said. "Sure, it's a stinking job and all, but heck, someone's gotta do it. But a pigman" — he gave me a wink — "dollar for dollar is worth more than two cowmen and two chickenmen any day. If it weren't for me and my brothers and my dad and your dad pushing, we wouldn't have half the operation this one is. But we know the difference between chicken-feed operations and reality. There's something in our blood that tells us how to operate big time. Oh, you'll hear differently from the Hufers and the Wipfs — even from some of the Wolners who'd like to see us in the dirt, but me and my brothers — and your dad too — are the brains of this farm. If we weren't this big into pigs, Rockyview would bury us. But Flat Willow is going to be a strong farm. We have the best fieldman in charge of the fields, and a heck of a good pigman in charge of the pigs."

That sneaky Kleinser Thom. He was talking politics. That clan of his never for a minute gave up on trying to schmier you over to their clan.

"You know," Thom continued, as if talking to an adult, "at Rockyview people always tried to push me and my brothers to the dirt. Always trying to dig up the past. You know the rumours they told about Chuck — you were old enough — about shipping those pigs and keeping the money under the table, and flying to Vancouver with a whore when he was supposed to be in the hospital. Oh, and then there's the one about him being involved with the Mafia. Don't believe that stuff, Peter. Just throw those rumours out of your head, because they just aren't true."

A bad patch is better than a hole. Right, Thom?

"Thom?"

"Yes?"

"What were those problems really about with that poor man?"

Thom whirled around. "Is your Josh-Vetter starting that crap again?"

Boy, he was edgy!

"No. I heard you talk at the fruit truck," I said quickly. "And I was wondering."

Thom shook his head. "That's another one they're gonna load on my brothers forever, claiming Sommel and Joel stole that neighbour's gun."

"Did they, Thom?"

"Hell, no, Peter. That lunatic Pierre over at the Longmans' farm stole it. Sorry about telling you all this, because kids shouldn't be pulled into that kind of crap. But I figure if nobody's told you the truth yet, it's high time you knew. If you never hear both sides of the story, you'll stay ignorant about it forever. That man was crazy, if you ask me, walking all over the land, pulling fox-trappers' traps out of the ground. He wasn't just some poor guy you have to feel sorry for — he was nuts, that's what. He got mad if you killed a fly. You should've seen him when Sommel and Joel butchered pigs that day. The neighbours had to come and get him. Threatened to shoot my brothers, that's what he did. Just like those city slickers you read about, chaining themselves to meat trucks and shit. But you pick up one end of the stick, and you pick up the other one too. That's a law that won't bend over for anybody. It doesn't matter who or what you are.

"And that's why people think it was Sommel and Joel who stole that gun, so that lunatic wouldn't come after them with the neighbour's gun. I say being threatened with a bullet was reason enough for stealing it, but my brothers say they didn't do it. Yet, nobody believes them. That's how it always is. Sure, jump on the scapegoats of the past."

We walked down the middle walkway of the farrow barn. The sows flapped their long ears, and grunted and heaved inside the farrow crates. Under their feet and to the sides, litters of piglets squealed and sniffed about on the Tenderfoot brand slats. I stopped at one crate and reached down. The whole litter ran toward my hand, trying to sniff it. Their dark eyes were like a bunch of moving buttons, and their pink snouts were soft and warm and wet.

I hesitated a little before asking, but then I just blurted it out. "Thom, was that poor man really able to tame the sows as people said?"

Thom laughed. "You know, as crazy as the man was, he did have some effect on the sows. I wouldn't say he tamed them, mind you. That's a stretched one. But he did have some weird way" — he took off his black hat and scratched his head — "he had some crazy chant that calmed them down."

"Did you see it?" I asked.

"Well, actually, I didn't. I wasn't here much. I was with the building crew most of the time."

"Who saw it, then?" I persisted.

"You don't believe it?"

"Why should I?"

Thom frowned. His intense blue eyes searched my face. "What have my brothers ever done to you, anyway, Peter, that makes you hate them so much?" he said.

I shrugged. "I don't hate them."

"You don't?"

"No," I said.

But Thom must've seen the lie on my face, or he knew more than he let on. He put his arm around my shoulder. "You can tell me," he said softly. "It's Chuck you hate. Right?"

I nodded.

"You still haven't forgiven him for tricking you into believing your mother had died?"

I nodded again.

Thom was quiet for a moment. He stared at the farrow crate in front of us, then at the ceiling. "Heck, I know my brother has a little problem with...well, you know...some people have that problem, causing them to be jackasses," he said, giving me a playful punch. "But geez, Peter. What are you? Twelve? Thirteen? How often do you pray? When you get up in the morning and when you go to sleep at night, right? Think about it. That's what?...730 times a year you ask God to forgive you as *you* forgive others their trespasses. Have you ever thought about that? Put that good head of yours in gear for a minute" — he tapped my head — "and do some calculating. Add up a few years of praying. You know, that's a lot of empty promises to God. And He's probably saying to Himself: 'Uh oh, here's that lying Wolner Peter on his knees again. I don't believe that boy any more. Every day, he crucifies my son Jesus anew, by telling all those lies. Every day, he's trying to throw away one end of the stick while refusing to let go the other end.'

I mean, Peter, how can you expect God to start taking *you* seriously and heal you of stuff that happened in the past, if you don't start with yourself?"

I held back a tear. Thom spoke roughly, but he usually made sense. And just as Dorothea had married into the Kleinser clan, Thom had married into the Wolner clan. "Blood is thicker than water," people said.

I told Thom a few more things, and he listened intently. I knew I didn't hate Thom.

Chapter Twelve

After supper, I slunk away before anyone had a chance to mention work. If I was needed somewhere, nobody would be able to blame me for not being there because I didn't know about it. It had come to this. But you couldn't speak your thoughts right out and say, "Mother, can I be excused? I'm hoping to meet a girl at a shack." She would have had a heart attack. "What? A twelve-year-old boy alone with a girl? And from out there yet, where the wolves are?" "Well, yes, Mother, but there aren't any wolves. There's only one gray cat."

But Tessa wasn't at the shack. This time I didn't wait, but set out toward her farm right away. Walking between the hills, where the air was still and perfumed with sagebrush, was like stepping into the hot bakehouse in the kuchel when the women baked bread and zwieback, and my black pants and yellow checkered shirt were sticky with sweat. I'd quenched my thirst with cool watermelon and a glass of frosty root beer before supper. Now I wished I could plunge into a cool dugout. Heck, I might not even bother taking my clothes off. I walking past a rosebush, which made me think of making a pfeifela to attract Tessa's attention if I saw her, so I ran back to the shack and cut a stem as thick as a fountain pen off a willow. Through the trees, I saw the red Supercab truck leaving Flat Willow — travelling along the gravel road like a Hollander. Someone was in a terrible hurry.

On the way back around the hills, I made a surface cut three inches from the end of the stem, then tapped a little on the bark with my pocket knife to loosen it. In a minute I had stripped the tube off the stem. The idea was to notch a little sound hole near one end, then to fashion a three-quarter-moon-shaped plug from the naked stem and fit it in front of the hole. With the tube pushed halfway back onto the stem, the thing was supposed to whistle. The boys and I had made plenty of stem whistles at Rockyview. Hufer Miechel and I had used them to chase off cattle rustlers and wild beasts in the foothills.

But for some reason my pfeifela didn't pfeif. I could have done better with just my lips. Sometimes you had to tinker with the plug, making it smaller so more air could pass through, or make a new one because too much air was passing through.

A vehicle hummed somewhere. At first I thought it might be coming down the winding road leading to Flat Willow, but then I saw the watermelon truck hurtle down the road in the hills, trailing a cloud of dust. I crouched behind a thorny buffaloberry shrub, working frantically to get my whistle going, and dropped the plug in the effort. It sprang off the dry grass like a hayhopper. By the time I'd made a new plug, I had cut my thumb and was cursing like a welt-pengel and the truck had pulled into the yard. Tessa and her cousin bounced out. My stomach felt like a swarm of bees again when I saw Tessa. Why, the two of us practically knew each other. But then I thought about what Thom had told me about Pierre, and I wasn't so sure I knew her. Why hadn't she told me about the trouble at the pigbarns? What about the gun? Maybe I'd be better off forgetting about her, go back to Flat Willow and read a little in Olvetter's new Chronicle book.

Tessa and her cousin had gone into the farmhouse. What now? Would they come out again? Or was the evening pretty much kaput? I stood like a patient cow for five or twenty minutes — it was hard to tell. I wished the watermelon woman would leave. Alone. Why did people barge in all the time? I'd had to sneak around like a cat in the tall grass to get this far, and even this opportunity was being stolen from me. But the watermelon woman didn't leave. The two came out of the house, laughing about something. When I saw them, my pulse, which was going at a pretty good clip already, throttled up some more. They were practically naked, wearing just bathing suits, and were carrying towels. I knelt behind the bush, gawking like the first time I'd seen a television in Lethbridge. They walked across the yard and disappeared behind the machine shed and a row of caragana.

They probably had a dugout there, something Flat Willow didn't have yet. We got by with three good wells. My father had shown them to me on Monday, and he'd told me they would dig a standby dugout after harvest.

A thought occured to me then, and I almost laughed out loud. "But Father, it was so shrecklich hot," I might say afterwards. "I almost died from heat after working so hard with the geese. So I ran to the neighbour's place for a swim in their dugout." "Okay then, Peter. I understand."

No way. I'd get a devil of a licking, as sure as the sun came up in the east. Boys never swam in the dugout with the girls. Actually, the girls weren't allowed to swim in the dugout, period. The reason for it was sort of vague, but I knew it had to do with sin. The most I'd seen were the girls' bloomers on windy days.

I looked around. I knew that the devil wasn't far away, probably behind a bush somewhere. For half a second I thought maybe I should pray a little to chase him off. *Geh weck vu mir, du Sotan!* But then, something in me didn't really want to send him away just yet. Maybe later, after I'd seen whatever I might see behind the shrubs, I could tell the devil to get lost. The thought of what I might see made my head reel. I slunk along the little ravine and in a few minutes I was at the machine shed. The two were splashing and laughing already in the dugout. The gray cat suddenly darted from behind tall kochia weeds in front of me. I saw an opening in the caragana. The water was a mere twenty feet behind the trees. Beside the opening, the wreck of an old roof with holes in the gable stuck out of the grass. I crouched beside it and, pressing against the gable, slowly eased my way toward the opening.

I thought about it later, how, when an alarm clock goes off, you hover between sleep and awakening for a few seconds, and you don't know what's making the sound. When I heard the buzzing sound I thought at first it was a power pole humming like they do in the wind. Then I heard a sharp whine near my ear. I looked back. A storm of wasps or bees was whirling out of a hole in the gable. I froze.

At the first sting on my arm, I leaped up like a jackrabbit, and let out a scream. I could go only two ways. Behind me was the swarm and in front of me the opening. The swarm started toward me. I crashed through the opening. Another wasp stung my arm. Where I'd heard or read about running for cover in the water, I didn't know. The main thing was that I remembered. At the water, I leaped and landed with a terrific belly flop. Tessa and her cousin were somewhere to my right. One of them shrieked. The coolness of the dugout shot through me like electricity. When I came up for air, water was flowing off the peak of my katus like a waterfall. The whole world swam in front of me. The two English people were creating a whirlpool in the dugout.

"PETER! SPLASH AROUND! MAKE A LOT OF SPLASHES!"

Lord, I splashed. I splashed like a human egg beater or something. I don't know how long I churned around there, but when I finally stopped, my head was spinning and the watermelon woman was beside me.

"It's all right now," she said, holding my arm. "You can stop. They're gone."

She led me to the shore and I sat down on the grass. Tessa waded out of the water and knelt down in front of me.

"Peter, you crazy knucklehead," she said, grabbing my shoulders. "You should have walked around the shrubs."

I rubbed my eyes. I looked first at Tessa, then at her cousin standing a few feet behind her. Hell, they didn't even realize I'd been spying on them.

"How many stings did you get?" the watermelon woman asked.

"Two," I said, pushing up my shirt-sleeve, which had unrolled in the water. The sting was swollen.

"You were lucky the dugout was close," Tessa said.

"Yeah," I said, gazing sheepishly at the ground. For a long, tense and embarrassing minute, nobody spoke. I couldn't just keep staring at the ground. I had to look somewhere. The watermelon woman walked closer, and towered over Tessa. My eyes practically fastened themselves onto her. I figured a blind man would have got his eyesight back right on the spot. The blue thing on her was hardly bigger than a postage stamp, and I thought the thin laces might break any minute, and her breasts would spring out. The pictures in Sears catalogue that Hufer Miechel and I had stared at intently and with great interest were nothing compared to this.

She gave me a suspicious grin, and picked up a towel.

Tessa turned to her cousin. "Holly, what might thou do?" she said in a singsong, drawn-out sort of voice. "A handsome cowboy cometh charging through the bush on a midsummer eve, and he jumpeth into the water to cool off, but now he hath been turned into a wet frog."

Holly squinted and contorted her face. "Well, thou dost know the remedy for that," she said in the same voice.

"If I kisseth him, might he turn back into a handsome cowboy once more — is that what thou sayesth?"

My pulse quickened.

"Yes," the watermelon woman said, wrapping her towel around herself.

"Shouldst I risk it?" Tessa said with a straight face.

"Me thinks thou should."

I sat like a real frog on a log.

"Close thy eyes, my handsome frog," Tessa said.

I closed my eyes and waited. The kiss was quick, and light as goose down, and the smell of dugout mud was in my nose.

Chapter Thirteen

I sat on the steps of the farmhouse deck. Tessa and her cousin had gone inside. They had suggested I take my clothes off so they could pop them into the dryer downstairs, but I'd said, "No way, they'll dry by themselves."

Tessa came out of the house with two glasses and a bottle of pop. She had on blue jeans and a blue shirt with shiny pearl buttons. Her hair was tied in a pony-tail.

"Want some root beer?" she said.

"Yeah."

She sat down beside me. I could smell perfume. She handed me the glasses, then twisted off the plastic cap on the bottle. As she poured, she gave me a long steady smile. Then she set down the bottle and moved real close to me. I didn't mind. She touched my pant leg.

"Gee, you're drying fast," she said.

"Yeah. It's the sun," I said, and took a sip of the pop. I loved that first swallow. The root beer fizzed and exploded in my mouth. I thought about The Cowboy Kid, and grinned.

Tessa lowered her head and looked sideways at me. "Holly said you might have been spying on us," she said.

I said nothing.

"Were you?"

I could see a lie coming up. I shrugged.

"Were you, Peter?" She was serious.

There was a minute of silence. "I just wanted to see you," I said.

Tessa sat up straight. "I'm really glad you came," she said. "I wished we could have stayed at your colony longer today. But Holly was furious at the preacher for hurting that boy. She said that preacher is bad — he's a tyrant."

"Don't say that," I said.

"Why not? The man was cruel. He is too a tyrant."

"NO, TESSA. Please don't say that. He's the preacher. God might...."

Tessa gave her head a toss, and her pony-tail slapped against my shoulder. "Do you think they'll still buy Holly's peaches after playing the radio so loud?"

"I don't know. I wouldn't be surprised if they didn't. Radios and music are forbidden, you know."

Tessa frowned. She took a long swallow from her glass. "Oh, well," she said. "Peter, but you are so lucky to have all those sisters. Your sister Lisbeth, she's cool."

"Cool?"

Tessa laughed. "Yeah, cool — you know, super, great, a fine person."

"But she sure teases a lot," I said.

She turned toward me. "You know why your sisters tease you, Peter?"

"Why?"

"Because they love you, you knucklehead," she said, squeezing my hand. "They're crazy about you."

The screen door behind us opened and Holly walked across the deck. She was dressed like a cowgirl. Her brown hat had a very high crown and a flat brim that turned down a little in the front. And she wore blue jeans with little silver studs running down the sides of her legs. Even her shirt was fancy, with leather fringes hanging from the pockets. Her boots were tan-coloured and had little silver decorations near the tip. She looked beautiful.

"Well, I'm off," she said. "I'll be back in about two hours, sweetheart," she said to Tessa. "You have your cowboy to protect you till I get back." She winked at me.

Tessa stood up and the two hugged. Suddenly, I felt like a wheelbarrow loaded with cow manure for having spied on them.

Holly stepped in front of me and crouched down. Her face was close enough to make me feel dizzy. She smelled of shampoo and perfume. She placed one hand on my shoulder, and I trembled a little.

"So your family doesn't know you're here?" she said.

"No."

"And you're not afraid?"

"Heck, no."

"And you're not afraid Tessa and I might want a wild cowboy to keep us company on the way to BC on Saturday and decide to kidnap you?"

I smiled, pushing my tongue against the inside of my cheek. She read my thoughts. "And I have a feeling you little sneak would like that," she said, giving my nose a quick tap.

I nodded, and she laughed. But then she got serious and said, "Okay then, you make sure no harm comes to my cousin. She's the only one I have."

I nodded again.

Tessa and I watched her climb into the truck. She waved a few times as she drove off, and each time Tessa and I waved back.

"Isn't she the coolest?" Tessa said.

"Yeah," I said, and I doubted she knew how much I meant that.

Tessa touched my arm. "Peter. You're about dry enough," she said. "Just take off your shoes, and let's go inside. I want to show you our house."

I hesitated. "I can't."

"Why not, Peter?"

"I dunno."

I had never been inside an English person's house.

"Oh, come on, Peter," she said, taking my hand. "Your preacher man isn't here."

I pulled off my shoes and socks and laid them beside my katus on the steps. The first room was like a porch. Clothes hung on hooks above a long shoe rack. Beside the door, an aluminum baseball bat leaned against the wall. I'd never seen an aluminum baseball bat. I picked it up. If someone — someone who wasn't a pacifist — were inclined to beat someone up, this would be the tool to do it with. Straight ahead of me, stairs went down to a basement, and right beside them, another stairway went up. I smelled flowers. To the left, and up a couple of stairs, the room opened into a bigger room with a mustard green fridge and a white stove beside kitchen cupboards. I'd never thought about it much, but all the kitchen area Flat Willow houses had was a sink near the hallway, because people went to the kuchel to eat. When my mother and my sisters cooked at home, they used our little electric cooker. At Rockyview there'd been even less — just a flat washstand to stand the wash-basin on. And now we had showers in the houses, while at Rockyview the showers were still communal.

Tessa showed me the entire house. There was actually a lot of room. From the outside, the house had looked much smaller. She showed me the room in the basement where Pierre had lived. Her Uncle Frank and Aunt Mae, who had driven to Winnipeg for summer holidays, lived upstairs. In their bedroom, among several framed pictures on a large drawer-cabinet, was a photo of a nun. I had seen nuns in the hospital in Lethbridge once. I'd been afraid of them. Their black dresses and black kerchiefs reminded me of funerals and graves. Tessa noticed me staring at the picture.

"That's Uncle Frank's sister in Ontario," she said. "You don't swear in front of her. She's very religious."

I thought for a minute. "Are you religious, Tessa?"

She gave me a reserved look. "Why do you ask?"

"Because...you gotta get baptised someday and get

extremely religious," I said. "If you don't, God will...I dunno...I just hope *you* — and Holly too — don't have to go to hell at the end of the world."

"What makes you think we'd go to hell?"

I shrugged.

"Don't worry about us, Peter," she said. "We won't go to hell. And for your information, Pastor Waldner, we're already baptised."

"Oh," I said. That was spooky. I'd always thought you had to be eighteen to get baptised. I'd have to ask my father about that.

Tessa showed me a small room lined with bookshelves. There was even a bookshelf in one little hallway upstairs. Most of the books belonged to Tessa's Aunt Mae, who was a teacher.

"She's the one who turned me into a bookworm," Tessa said.

"How many books have you read, anyway?" I asked.

"About five thousand."

"Really? Five thousand? Holy cow."

"You shore are a gullible ol' cowboy there," Tessa said in an imitation western accent. "Bin riden' the range too long all by yur lonesome, ah reckon." And she laughed. Then I laughed too. I wished I could stay with her for a whole year.

After the tour of the house, Tessa said, "Come sit in the living-room." The room was opposite the kitchen and there was no wall in between. It had a red carpet that reminded me of a shaggy dog. In the corner stood a big television. I wondered if Tessa would switch it on.

"Sorry about the mess in here," she said, taking a stack of magazines and cookbooks off the low glass-topped table in the middle of the room. "Aunt Mae has been away for a week and Dad isn't a very good housekeeper. But he went to Calgary for business and won't be back till next week."

I sat down on the couch. "What about your mother?" I said. "Cleaning the house is a mother's job."

Tessa placed the magazines in a basket in the kitchen. She stepped in front of the fridge and paused with her hand on the handle. She was quiet for a moment.

"My mom's gone," she said.

"Oh," I said. "When did she die?"

"She didn't. She left us."

A chill went down my neck. "When is she coming back?" I asked.

"She's not coming back, Peter."

I didn't catch on right away. "But how could she be married — ?" Then I caught on.

Tessa took a plate with half a watermelon on it from the fridge. She peeled off a thin plastic sheet, then grabbed a knife from a drawer.

"Mom ran off with Mr. Clements' rich brother," she said. "But I don't like talking about her any more. She's not coming back, anyway. I just hope when we move to Calgary and my dad is the owner of The Steak House Restaurant that he and his uncle Calvin are buying, everything will get better for him. Just like it was before. Dad had to get out of farming and sell most of the land because he couldn't keep up with the payments. But I will never give up on my dad, I don't care what happens."

I didn't know what to say. Tessa shrugged and gave me a weak smile, which I took to mean, "everything will be fine."

She walked across the rooms with the plate of watermelon slices. "Holly is so cool," she said, placing the plate onto the low glass-topped table. "She brings fruit from British Columbia every summer. We get ours free. Holly usually stops at roadsides and sells to people passing by. It's her summer job, for some of her university money."

"Why? Does it take money to go to university?" I asked.

"Of course, Peter."

"Are you going to go to university?"

"I sure hope so," Tessa said, sitting down beside me. "Are you?"

"No. I'll go to just grade eight."

"Why only that far?"

"I don't know. After grade eight we go on the field or to the stocks." I picked up a watermelon slice.

"There's so much to learn in university," Tessa said. "Everybody should go. It's not fair that you can't."

"That's all right."

She picked up a slice of watermelon too. "You know what you should do?" she said.

"What?"

"You should run away from Flat Willow when you're eighteen or something and go to university."

"I could never run away from my mother."

"But in university you could study whatever you want. Holly is going to be an engineer. Hey, you could study to be an artist."

"A real artist?"

"Sure."

"Wow!"

"Yeah."

I shook my head. "It could never be, though. Our colonies are the arks of the world. If a person gets born in the ark, he's never allowed to leave because God would never forgive him."

Tessa stared at the ceiling for a minute. "Want some potato chips?" she asked.

"Sure." I liked potato chips.

Tessa walked to the cupboards and opened a door. A few bags tumbled out.

"Damn," she said. "All we have left is plain."

I liked plain, but I said nothing. I'd eat whatever she gave me. She pulled out a bowl from another cupboard.

Then I thought about the gun. It was the first time I had actually thought about it since coming here. I hesitated before saying anything. Tessa had acted so spooky at the shack when we talked about Pierre, and I didn't want her to get scary again. But the question kept cooking in my mind.

"It sure is strange about that gun the boys found," I said finally, watching Tessa jiggle chips into the bowl.

She turned toward me suddenly, almost knocking the bowl off the kitchen table. She was quiet for a minute, and she held the half-empty chip bag at her side. She opened her mouth to say something, but didn't. I could tell from the way her eyes got big and her face twitched that she'd become spooky again.

"I mean, there's a rumour that the pigman's brothers stole the gun," I said. "But my sister's man Thom, he says it's a bunch of lies."

Tessa placed her hand to her throat and swallowed hard. "Sorry, Peter, but it's true," she said.

"How do you know?"

She walked across the room and set the bowl on the low table. She sat down on the couch beside me. "See, Pierre got mad at Mr. Clements for giving them the gun to shoot his rabbits that he had tamed in the coulee. Then, when Mr. Clements asked for his gun back, the men in the pigbarns got mad. And they got Mr. Clements drunk and stole it out of his truck, hoping to blame it on Pierre."

"How do you know that?"

Her eyes narrowed. "My dad told me."

"Where does Mr. Clements live?" I asked.

"About two miles north of Flat Willow," Tessa said, and the troubled look on her face got worse. "Mr. Clements is scary. You know, I've actually gone to the shack a few times to read when my dad had to go somewhere quick, in case Mr. Clements came by. It's a good hideout."

My scalp crawled. "Why, is he a murderer?"

Tessa sat down beside me. She shook her head. "No, silly, but he acts weird. Every time he sees me, he tells me I'm pretty...and other weird stuff like that. You don't want to meet him when he's drunk."

"What does he do?"

Tessa made a crisscross motion with her hands. "Peter, he has never done anything, okay? He just acts weird. We have better things to talk about than Mr. Clements."

"Do you hate him?"

She nodded, and her lips turned down slightly. I thought she might start crying. I wanted to tell her to let go both ends of the stick and to stop crucifying Jesus every day, but I didn't think she would understand. If Thom was here, he could explain it better.

"I used to hate him a lot more," she said. "I hated him for his brother, for bringing him here. My dad says Mr. Clements' brother stole Mom away."

I wondered if she hated Mr. Clements as much as I had hated the pigman. For a minute neither of us spoke. We both took some potato chips. I thought more about what Thom had said.

"My sister's man said Pierre wanted to shoot the pigman's brothers when he saw them butcher pigs one time. Did he really?"

Tessa spoke in a surly tone. "Yeah, Pierre was touchy when he saw dying animals and blood. Pigs have a lot of blood. It spurts out of their throats and gurgles like they're drowning in it. It's awful. When Pierre saw that, he got mad as thunder."

Something wasn't right.

"Who told your father that the boys stole the gun?" I asked.

Tessa gave me an impatient look. "Who else but the men in the pigbarn would've stolen it? They were the only ones around that night. It was on one of those weekends when your building crew drove back to Alberta. They were drinking in the pigbarn, and the next day the gun was gone out of Mr. Clements' truck."

I shook my head. "But Tessa, it's easy to see who stole the gun."

"Who?"

"Pierre. You said he was mad at the boys for shooting the rabbits. And maybe he wanted to steal it to shoot Samuel and Joel like he said he would. So maybe he stole the gun while the boys were in the barns?"

"That's impossible. Pierre wasn't home that night. He and Uncle Frank had gone camping."

I took a few chips from the bowl. "Why did he go out in the blizzard, anyway?"

"I told you before, Peter. Nobody knows. Pierre often went for long walks across the fields. But I can tell you, on the night when the gun disappeared, Pierre wasn't home."

"What did he do out there?"

"He tried to imitate the calls of the coyotes and foxes. He said he was going to tame a coyote."

"Really?"

"Yeah. Before he moved here, he lived at Hudson Bay with Uncle Frank's brother Earl. Pierre had an Indian friend called The-One-with-the-Voices who taught him how to make animal sounds. That's how he could tame the rabbits."

"My sister's man says Pierre pulled traps out of the ground that a fox-trapper had placed." I was direct.

Tessa held up her index finger. "One time," she said. "One time he went after some traps, that all. You have to understand, Pierre was an animal-lover. He didn't even know it, but he was an animal activist. But he found traps only once. Do you know how hard they are to find out there?"

I said nothing.

Tessa got up from the couch and walked to the TV cabinet. She opened a drawer and pulled out a large photo album.

"So you want to play detective, huh?" she said, frowning. "Well, Mr. Sherlock Holmes, I'll tell you about Pierre." She sat down beside me and flipped open the back cover of the album. "See, there's Pierre, a few months before he died."

I leaned over and looked from one picture to another. Pierre was a large and square-shouldered man with long gray hair. In all the pictures except one, he had the same withdrawn expression. In that one picture, he was sitting on the ground, smiling. About three feet in front of him, rabbits were nosing in a patch of oats.

"He doesn't look retarded," I said.

"If you look closely, you can tell," Tessa said. "But Pierre didn't have Down's Syndrome. It's not even right to say that he was retarded, because he really wasn't. He was just...you know...poor in his thinking, like you say. He couldn't think things through."

"My sister's man says Pierre was a lunatic."

Tessa said nothing. She flipped a few pages. A lot of photos went by.

"Was he a lunatic?"

"No more than you're a lunatic, Peter," she said, without looking up. "Are you a lunatic for wanting to come and see me, and risk getting a beating from your dad?"

I shrugged. I didn't think wanting to kill someone and running to the neighbour's farm were the same thing.

"Uncle Frank and Aunt Mae sort of adopted Pierre two years ago when Earl died," Tessa continued. "Pierre had lived with Earl and his wife since he was nine years old."

She put her finger on a picture of a boy sitting on a horse beside a car with round fenders. Under the picture, it said *1954.*

"That's Pierre in Ontario, before Uncle Frank's brother adopted him," she said.

In another picture, Pierre was squinting into the sun. Behind him was a long wooden barn.

"That barn burned down," Tessa said.

"Holy cow."

She bit her lip. "Pierre was the one who set it on fire."

My legs seemed to float away from me.

"Pierre got mad at his grandfather one day and kicked

over a coal oil lamp and the whole barn went ablaze. Not a single cow was saved. Even Pierre's horse died in the fire."

"Geez," I said. "That's terrible."

"Yeah. His grandfather was a drinking man. He used to beat up Pierre. See, Pierre didn't have a father because his father went to fight in World War Two just before he was born. The mother was a teenager, and she died when Pierre was born. So the grandparents adopted him."

I was clawing at the couch. "I hope that grandfather went to hell."

Tessa slapped my arm. "Peter! Don't say that."

She closed the photo album, then turned toward me. "I'm sorry I slapped you," she said. "But you're so...that was such a cruel thing to say. I wish I hadn't told you *this* much. I wanted you and I just to talk about nice things this time," she squeezed my hand, "I mean, there are so many good things to talk about. I don't know why Pierre's past keeps creeping up all the time."

She picked up the photo album and took it back to the TV cabinet. "So let's promise right now, Peter Waldner," she said, "you'll keep your big Sherlock Holmes mouth shut, and I won't say another word about Pierre."

"Okay," I said.

"See, I almost told you all about Pierre at the shack," Tessa said. "But you were already so spooked about everything I'd told you, I was afraid you'd run away from me again."

"I didn't run away from you, Tessa."

"Are you sure?"

"Yes."

"Positive?"

"How do you mean?"

"Well," she said slowly, lifting her chin high. "I kind of saw you the first time" — she poked my arm with her finger— "you spied on me."

"You saw me that time?"

"Well, I didn't know it was you I saw sneaking away

among the willows, but I figured out later that it was you. Who else would have known to bring the books back? Think I'm dumb?" She boxed my arm and laughed. "Peter Waldner, I think you are the sneakiest person in the world. Look at you. You told Holly and me you'd get a licking from both your dad and your teacher if they found you here."

I laughed dryly. "But why didn't you tell me before that you knew I'd run away the first time?" I said.

"You were spooked, remember?"

"But you could have told me that."

"Yeah, right, and embarrass you?"

"You spooked me, Tessa, but I wouldn't have been embarrassed."

"Why did I spook you, anyway?"

"Because you talked like an adult, and you read all those difficult books. You seemed — I don't know — I didn't like talking about a man who froze."

"Oh, I see. And now you're the one who's asking the questions," she said in a sing-song voice. "I see." She lay back against the couch.

"And you reminded me so much of my sister Sara. She's fifteen already."

"Well, I am almost thirteen, Peter," she said, pushing out her chest toward me and blinking rapidly. I knew about that look. Sara had told me how girls flirt. The way Tessa had looked at me and said, "Oh, I see," was what you had to watch for. Good thing Sara had told me about the gum part too. "When you give a girl a piece of gum, that's a good time to kiss her," she'd said. All that listening and storing stuff in my head was going to come in handy, after all.

Tessa edged very close to me. "What's the matter, Peter? You're shaking," she giggled.

I looked at my hand. I *was* shaking. I put my hand into my damp pocket and pulled out the packet of gum. It was wrecked.

"Looks like your gum's kaput."

I looked at her eyes. They were big and shiny. Oh well, I'd have to do without the gum. She took my hand and puckered her lips. But then she suddenly exploded with laughter, and sort of rolled and bounced away from me, burying her face in the couch. I tried laughing too, but couldn't. I'd turned as serious as a preacher. When she was in front of me again I took a deep breath and lifted my hand to touch her shoulder and steer me toward her. My heart was pounding. But my hand stopped in mid-air and stayed there, shaking.

"Just close your eyes, cowboy. I'll go first," Tessa said.

I closed my eyes and felt her hand on my shoulder. I stopped breathing.

HONK HONK, HONK HONK HONK

What the devil? I leaped a foot off the couch. Tessa sprang up from the couch and ran across the room and kitchen to the door. I was right behind her.

"Who is it?" I said.

"It's Mr. Clements' truck."

A truck door slammed. Then another one slammed.

"He's with the fat pigman," Tessa said.

I panicked. Now what? If the pigman saw me here, he'd probably tell his brother, and his brother would tell my sister, and my sister would tell my mother, and my mother would tell my father, and boy oh boy, would I be in trouble.

Footsteps sounded on the deck. I moved behind the solid wood door, eying the closet nearby. Through the crack I could see the pigman sway up. He had to steady himself on the railing. Beside him trudged an English man with a haggard-looking face. He had eyebrows like caterpillars and his hair curled out the back of his oily cap like a duck-tail. An unlit cigarette dangled from his mouth.

"Your dad home?" Mr. Clements had a drawling voice.

"He's sleeping, Mr. Clements."

"Sleepin' this time of the ev'nin? Come on."

"He just came back from Regina. He was tired," Tessa said.

"Well, wake 'em up. Tell 'em it's my birthday. We gotta have a drink fer old time sake." Mr. Clements staggered and lurched, but he remained standing. Chuck was staring at my shoes and katus on the steps.

"You have a birthday every week, Mr. Clements," Tessa said.

"Well, tell 'em this time it's for real."

"My dad doesn't drink any more."

"Come on, pretty girl, tell 'em just one drink. Then he can go back to them A Ass meetens'."

"Go away, Mr. Clements." Tessa reached for the house door.

Mr. Clements moved forward. "Hey sweetheart, how about a kiss?"

The pigman laughed. "Well, I don't give a damn what you do, Ralph," he said. "I'm goin' for another rye. Do what you gotta do."

Tessa grabbed the wooden door and tried to close it, but Mr. Clements yanked open the screen door and his big hand shot between the door and the door frame.

"Peter Waldner, help me!" Tessa cried out. "Push against the door."

I flung myself against the door and pushed on the doorknob. Mr. Clements' huge arms were in the doorway. I could smell the whiskey on his breath. Behind him, the pigman was staggering away.

Tessa cried out, "Peter, what would The Cowboy Kid do?"

My head went into a spin. It was all happening so fast. The Cowboy Kid wasn't a real hero. He was just a scratchy-looking pencil drawing that came from my head. I'd never thought that anything he did would ever come true. He was made up. But this was happening for real. There was no time to think. Mr. Clements heaved at the door and, with a final burst, the door flew open. When I saw the look of fright on Tessa's face, and heard the thud as she crashed against the panelled wall, I saw red streaks shooting from the ceiling. And suddenly I *was* The Cowboy Kid. He was furious like dynamite. With muscles like a wildcat's, he snatched up the baseball bat. Mr. Clements tottered in the doorway.

The Cowboy Kid stood poised. This whiskey-drinker was going to catch it, all right. "Make one more step, you boozer, and I'll knock you unconscious."

Mr. Clements laughed. "Get lost, you pip-squeak," he said, and started toward Tessa.

That's when I charged with the baseball bat. At that moment I was no pacifist. I had travelled too far into the night to say a prayer. I was a warrior. A law-maker with a baseball bat. I took aim and whacked Mr. Clements a good one across the shins. He froze up, wincing with pain. His hands flew up in the air. I stood poised to hit him again.

"I'm leaven', kid, I'm leaven'," he said, backing up. "No need to get violent now. All I wanted was a kiss from the young lady." He stood for a minute in the doorway and fired a volley of swear words at Tessa and me, accusing us of shameful things. The words would've set a preacher's ears on fire. That man had the devil speaking right through him. He was worse than the pigman, even.

As soon as he had backed over the threshold, Tessa sprang up and slammed the door shut, then bolted the door. She leaned back against the door and let out a long sigh. "Lord God help us." Her voice wavered. "I'm glad we're moving away from that man."

When she flicked on the house light, I saw that her face completely paled. She trembled. When I took her hand, she leaned against my shoulder. I felt her warm tears come through my yellow checkered shirt. I knew I wouldn't pray that night.

Chapter Fourteen

My mother's face and kerchief were lit up at the ash barrel, and she poked at paint-splotched cardboard sheets and newspapers, guiding them slowly into the fire with a pitchfork. Other ash barrels were lit along the gravel road at the back of family units. Cinders, glowing like fireflies, curled up and away from the unithouses. A harvest moon peeked over the rooftop of the kuchel. I felt like The Cowboy Kid, riding into a strange new town, and I blinked hard as my eyes adjusted to the firelight.

"Oh, there you are, Peter," my mother said, smiling. I could tell she was in a good mood. "Been helping Chuck and the boys in the pigbarn again, have you?"

WHAT?

"It's good that you're helping out in the pigbarns when Thom is away," she said, "but you should see that your own work gets done first."

"How do you mean, Mother? Where did Thom go?"

She gave me a puzzled look. "Didn't the boys tell you in the pigbarn?" She laughed. "Thom had to rush Dorothea to Swift Current with the Supercab this evening. You'll be a vetter soon."

As I stood wondering which lie would be smaller — letting my mother believe I'd been in the pigbarns or telling her I'd been out walking in the hills — Sara walked up, carrying a box of paint-rags and linoleum scraps under her arm.

She grabbed my arm. "Where were you so long?"

"Walking in the hills," I said, and it wasn't really a lie. I *had* walked in the hills.

"Those hills at Rockyview must still be in your blood," my mother said, starting back to the house. "But, Peter, you should ask Father about those hills back there. I don't think they belong to Flat Willow. You might run into kidnappers out there. Be careful where you walk. The world out there is so evil these days. They will do anything."

Sara grabbed my arm before I could leave. "Josh-Vetter — and Jerg Wipf too — were wondering where you were," she said. "Why are you avoiding the boys? What ails you?"

She let the box slip from her arms to the plank under our feet, and tightened her grip on my arm. Good thing the wasp stings were on the other arm.

"We worry about you," she said. "I hope you don't start drinking like Jake. You aren't stealing wine from the coldroom and drinking it in the goosebarn, are you?"

What? Drink like Jake? I was only twelve.

Sara leaned close to smell my breath. "Peter, how come you smell of perfume?"

Geez, was there anything Sara didn't notice?

"Lisbeth sprayed me before supper," I lied. "She said I stank of pigs."

"Olvetter was also asking about you. He was wondering why you're sliding back on your promise to read the Chronicles."

"He said I promised?"

"Didn't you?"

"Not completely."

"He still misses Ankela," she said. "And for your information, you can't talk to people once they're in the grave."

I pulled free and said, "I'll go see him — tomorrow."

"Make sure," she said. I figured she took it upon herself to be the boss over everybody. After what had happened at Tessa's farm, I wished more than ever now that I could tell Sara about Tessa. But if I told her, my father would know in ten seconds.

Inside the house, I saw that they had already arranged the furniture and hung the curtains. The big rooms seemed to swallow up the furniture. The living-room at the end of the hallway had one lone table in the corner, a few chairs and two leatherette upholstered benches along the wall. In another corner, at the large window, two sewing machines were set up.

As I filled a cup at the drinkwater faucet, I heard Josh-Vetter's voice coming from the living-room in the connecting half-unit. "All I am saying, Zack, is try to send three or four of the fieldmen too. Harvest or not, you can not expect the women to do all the slaughtering by themselves. One of the boys — Jake — the least he can do is the chopping."

"I'll see what I can do," I heard my father say.

Before I had a chance to scoot down the basement, Uncle Josh appeared at the door, twirling his fedora on his hand. He stopped abruptly when he saw me.

"Whoa, whoa, Vettela," he said in not too kind a tone. "Jeepers, I thought I had me a helper. Did you forget we need to get ready for slaughtering ducks on Friday?"

I stared at the floor.

"Listen, kid. You're the gooseboy first, then the pigboy," he said, pointing his finger at me like a pistol. "I got nothing against you helping Chuck and Thom in the pigbarns in your spare time, but don't forget that you're my helper first. So make sure that tomorrow morning, right after breakfast, you're down in the goosebarn. We have plenty of work to do before Friday." Then he left.

I had forgotten about Petch from Moon Ranch Colony too. I stepped hesitantly into the doorway of my father's room, and I saw Petch sitting on a bench pulled close to the table, visiting with my father. He had a bottle of beer in his hand. He smiled when he saw me.

"Well now, here he is, a Vetter-to-be," he said in his

smooth voice. I felt good instantly. There was something very reassuring about that voice.

"Come now, sit down, Peter-Vetter," Petch said.

Gracious, everybody was into that vetter thing.

I sat down beside him on the bench. *The Western Producer* newspaper lay open on the table in front of my father, and he too had a bottle of beer.

My father smiled. "There's a little beer left," he said. "Do you want it?"

"Sure."

My father handed me the bottle with about an inch of beer in it. "Peter's been working," he said, and there was pride in his voice. "I saw him before supper, coming out of the pigbarns. He's been helping Chuck and the boys when he's not busy with the geese."

Oi yoi yoi!

"My dear heaven, that's good!" Petch said. He laid his right leg over his left knee and gave his wrist a flip, as if shaking a handkerchief or something. He had thin wrists. He hunched his body forward and rested his elbow on his knee. "That's what the community needs. Conscientious and reliable young people, who, when their own work is done, won't run off to God knows where, but will instead seek out other places in the community to give service. Such sound character as Peter here already demonstrates is one that ought to be applauded."

No answer is also an answer, right?

"When I was a lad like him," Petch was talking to my father, but looking at me, "we branched out from Montana to Moon Ranch. And as you know, my father was on the side that moved. Oh, I had big hopes that he would still be the sheepman at Moon Ranch. But God chose him to be preacher instead, and Wilhelm-Vetter asked to have me work with the chickens. Now, it's good that Peter-Vetter here has such great insight already that tells him to go, without having to be told, and help out where there is work. I mean, not all people recognize it that early. I sure didn't. But some people have to be coaxed, and told what to do practically every day."

Petch Petch. Jumpen Jack. Crimeny Crimeny.

"But I doubt you need to worry about Peter-Vetter here," Petch continued. "I mean, just look. Sure, he may not like the geese so terribly much, but does that stop him from going to work where he really enjoys it after his own work is done? Of course not. He's a true Gmanshofter. He's not like those who just like filling their stomachs at the table, and sit around on their rears, expecting the others to do all the work." He reached over and patted my head. "Don't stop doing what you're doing, boy," he said.

My father nodded proudly. I wondered if Petch's nose was plugged. If I smelled of pigs, then the sun also came up in the west. Either he was really stupid, or he was using his half-cooked riddles again, talking some strange kind of logic. But whatever it was, boy oh boy, would I work with gusto the next day!

* * * *

My main job was catching the ducks. Josh-Vetter and I had built a wooden stockrack that fit overtop the little chore trailer. A sheet of plywood nailed on top was the roof. When I crawled under the plywood to grope for their necks, the ducks crowded to the far end, fluttering up a storm of straw, dust and feathers. The ducks quacked loudly, but the drakes with their shadowy voices could only whisper their fear of the doom that hung heavily in the air. The smell was on my clothes, on the chopping block, and on the large patch of blood-jello under the wheel. My clothes and gum-rubber boots were sprinkled with blood. I wondered if Pierre would threaten to shoot me too if he were still here. I passed the ducks to Jake, who shoved them head-first into cone-shaped pails clasped to the rim of a metal wheel. The wheel was left over from the olden days. It had spokes, and the hub sat on a metal pole welded to a disc. There was so much blood on the ground, the disc was buried. Only the ducks' heads stuck out the bottom of the pails. The pails kept the blood off the feathers so they could be used for pillows and quilts. Jake slowly turned the wheel. It made a lazy squeak. One after another, he stopped the ducks at the block and chopped off the heads, throwing them into a five-gallon pail where they moved their beaks back and forth a few times, then lay still.

Between batches, I carried the heads into the steam-filled slaughterhouse. The old ladies scalded them, then rubbed off the feathers, cleaning them. A tubful of heads was waiting at the door for the cooks in the kuchel. Duck heads for supper was always a special treat. Kleinser Joel and Jerg Wipf's big brother Sappy steamed the ducks in a square box over a vat of boiling water. Five minutes of steam made it easy for the plucking crew of adult boys and girls — who sang hymns and chewed gum — to rub off the feathers. Then Josh-Vetter dipped them into a vat of hot wax a few times. When the wax was cold, chickenman Jerg, Speed Jahannes-Vetter and the German schoolteacher slowly peeled it off, pulling all the stubborn stubble feathers along with it. Further along, the hauswirt and the preacher, with my mother and the other ladies, cut the ducks open, pulled out the insides, cleaned them off, then threw them into cooling vats.

We killed batch after batch. When the trailer was empty, Jake and I climbed onto the chore tractor, and chugged off for another load from the barn.

My brother was in high spirits, and between batches he sang cowboy songs. His voice was loud and all over the road, but he tried anyway. His favourite song was "Blue Canadian Rockies". Someone had recently taught him a new one, and he sang that one too, about two cowboys named Buster Jake and Sandy Bob. Those two were tough as old shoes, and they rode out on the Sierra Plain or something, looking for calves to brand. After a week of branding, they wanted a day off, so they rode to town and got drunk in the saloon. On the way home, they met up with the devil and he told them he'd just come up from hell to gather some cowboy souls to take back to hell with him. But the two cowboys challenged the devil to a fight. They threw a loop out and roped him. Then they grabbed the branding irons and the dehorning saw, cut his horns off, and branded him up all over. Afterwards they tied him to a big black goat and left him there, wailing over the knots they'd tied in his tail.

I laughed all through the song.

"You must really like that song," Jake said, giving me a light punch.

"Yeah, it's funny."

"So you've quit running for preacher, huh?"

"I never ran for preacher," I said. "I just like the song."

"I wonder why."

"How do you mean?"

"It's about drinking, and about the devil. I mean, not even a week ago you were giving me hell for having a few drinks."

"But that's different, Jake. The song is...well, you know it's not true. And it's funny."

Jake twisted the cap off his second beer. He sidled up to the wagon and leaned against the stockrack.

"You know what that song is about, brother?"

"What?"

"I'm Buster Jake and you're Sandy Bob, and we're both fighting the devil."

"That's crazy."

"Oh no, it isn't. Everybody's doing battle with the devil in some way. See, I like my booze, and you little welt-geist" — he pointed his finger at me — "like sneaking away to the English neighbour."

My body went numb.

"Yeah, I know," he said. "Leaving your katus and shoes lying around on the neighbour's steps. That's real bright of you."

"It wasn't me."

"Oh, lie about it, yet."

I was silent.

"You know you're not supposed to go to the neighbour's farm by yourself, Sandy Bob," Jake said with a dry laugh. "What do you suppose Mother would say? Now, me drinking and you sneaking around with the world people — don't you think we're balancing two pails of water on the same yoke here?"

Jake had me in a corner. It was creepy how calmly he had done it.

"Did Chuck tell you what Mr. Clements did?" I asked.

"Aha, so you admit it," Jake said. "I got you this time, Cowboy. Chuck didn't actually know who it was, but you fell right into it." He laughed. "And you think you're the smart one."

"Jake, it's not funny what Mr. Clements did. He tore open the door, and he threw the neighbour's girl against the wall. And he wanted to...you know...he wanted to grab her and kiss her. She's just a girl — not even an adult yet. And she was crying, Jake. He's big, and rough."

Jake frowned. He stared at the bottom of the wagon and spit on the straw. "And Chuck? Where was he?"

"He didn't tell you? Chuck's a liar, Jake. You know what that fat bugger did? He just laughed and said, 'Do what you have to do, Ralph,' and he walked away for more booze."

Jake hit the stockrack with his fist. I hadn't seen that serious look on his face for a long time.

"Chuck is evil," I said. "He doesn't belong in the ark, Jake. He and Mr. Clements should get their rears kicked back to Russia."

"Did Ralph hurt the girl?" Jake asked.

"He might've. But I stopped him with a baseball bat."

"*You* did?"

"Yeah."

"Bull."

"I did. You can believe that."

Jake said nothing. I didn't think he believed me, either.

"Are you going to tell, Jake?"

Jake stayed quiet. He walked to the grass at the edge of the slaughterhouse and sat down. He chopped with the axe at the dirt in front of him. Then the timer went off for us to kill the next batch of ducks, so we emptied the pails and carried the ducks into the slaughterhouse.

We began filling the pails again with live ducks. As I passed the first duck to my brother, I said, "Jake, I hope you won't tell Father."

Jake remained quiet.

"Jake, are you?"

"Hell no," he said. "Everybody gets caught sooner or later all by themselves. Don't you know anything?"

Jake didn't sing much after that, and he opened only two more beers. He offered me some and I drank three inches from a bottle. Then I felt dizzy and told Jake a few things. I even told a few lies, which he swallowed like Sunday noodle suppen. Jake wasn't baptised yet, and lying to someone like him was easy. He wasn't interested in hearing about Pierre or about the gun, though. He said everybody already knew that Kleinser Sommel and his brother Joel had stolen it.

"But you really saw the watermelon woman's breasts?" he asked.

"I saw everything, Jake. She was completely naked."

Jake shook his head. "The devil's really going after you, brother," he said, giving me a light punch. "You'd better be heating those branding irons soon." And he laughed.

Chapter Fifteen

Saturday was another hot day. Even in the morning, the sun was a fiery eye in the sky that seemed to focus on one spot like rays through field glasses. Tessa had told me about the thinning ozone layer when I said she smelled nice from her suntan lotion.

"What will happen when it's all gone?" I had asked.

She'd thought about it for a minute. "Well, the scientists say it's not too late yet."

"But what would happen?"

"Some pretty scary stuff."

"Will it be the end of the world?"

"Maybe," she'd said.

The work in the houses was done, and now it was harvest time. The combines crawled round and round in the field near the truck scale, feeding the swaths into the front, and shooting the empty straw and chaff out the back. The air was hazy from combine dust, and the smell of diesel smoke hung over Flat Willow.

In the slaughterhouse, women packed ducks into freezer bags and Josh-Vetter and I hauled them across the yard, one trailer after another, piling them into the walk-in locker in the kuchel. When my uncle opened the freezer door, a blast of winter shot out. He flicked the switch to shut the fans off, and slipped a sheepskin coat over his regular clothes. For a moment, after being in the heat outside, the freezer was a refreshing place to step into. It felt dangerously good.

"But you can get sick from the drastic changes in temperature," Josh-Vetter said. "If you get too much cold so quickly, you could die just like that, so just bring them to the door, Pete. I'll pack 'em in."

The shelves in the freezer were nearly empty.

"Will they ever be full?" I asked. The freezers seemed so huge.

"Just wait," Josh-Vetter said. "By December, it'll be stocked to the ceiling."

At that very moment, a barnful of fattening chickens was eating, drinking and gossiping politics with their neighbours, unaware of chickenman Jerg sharpening *his* axe. So were the geese. While they were enjoying cool water at the troughs, Josh-Vetter was planning where he would pile them. Those that didn't fit into the locker were sold to people in nearby towns. In the pigbarns too, Chuck and Thom probably had a few sows enclosed in a special pen already and were fattening them to make lard and swine wurst and ribs and hams and kreipen and other good things we made out of pigs in November. Even the four or five steers in the little cowshed by the side of the pigbarns, who were at that moment chewing barley and guzzling water, would end up in the freezer eventually.

The Bible said God had made different plans. Animals didn't need to worry about their souls. In fact, it never said that they had souls. Their job was to be ruled by humans and get fed loads of good feed from Cargill and Burns to fatten them up. All they had to do was take a few steps and open their mouths to get it. But in the end, they got butchered and eaten. The plan for people was to sweat for their food, and be fruitful. But people, had reason to worry. They had one chance to live either a good or bad life and then die, and forever have a huchzeit in heaven with God and Jesus and all the angels, or roast forever with the devil and his demons in hell, where even a single drop of water would be refused. That's why I knew that someday before I died, I would need to get seriously religious.

But today I had other plans. It was easy for Olvetter to wish for the end of the world. He'd had his chance. What did he care? If I was his age, I too would welcome the end of the world. I'd often grübled about that. I figured that when Judgement Day came, children would be cheated. They'd never have the chance to become the electrician, the plumber, the cowman, the fieldman, or anything like that. It would be like ploughing under a crop of tomatoes before they even had a chance to bloom.

I had talked that over seriously with Hufer Miechel once when we rode Madeline in the foothills. "Why would God want to come down and destroy these beautiful hills? Why couldn't He just forget about the things He had said in the Bible and make up another plan?"

But Miechel had looked uneasily up to the sky and said, "Don't talk like that, Wolner Peter. It's dangerous. It's our fault. We sinned. If Adam and Eve hadn't listened to the snake and eaten the apple, God would never have said He would burn the world."

I thought, surely, if Adam and Eve hadn't done it, then one of the thousands of people after them eventually would've. Esau would surely have done it. He was such a fool, selling his birthright to his younger brother Jakob for a little lentil dish. When he came home that night after hunting all day without any luck, he'd have walked straight to that apple tree and plucked off an apple. And I didn't think God could've trusted all those heathens with their idols and false gods, either, to stay away from the apple tree. Especially in those drought years when the Egyptians had nothing to eat but dried corn. Wouldn't they have wanted to try something a little different for a change, to loosen their stool a little? Apples were good for that. In the winter, when we ate a lot of white bread and pork, but not a lot of fresh vegetables, I was often plugged up. But when the hauswirt brought a truckload of BC apples from Calgary — hallelujah!

But I knew these thoughts came to me straight from the

devil down in hell, so I shoved them down into the deepest rootcellars of my mind and shut the lights off.

By half-to-nine lunch the ducks were all packed away. I walked through the kitchen area. The cooks were already preparing for dinner. Wipf Sanna-Pasel, the head cook, asked Esther Wipf, one of the week's cooks, to check the water temperature in the stainless-steel cooking vat. When Esther lifted the lid, the steam rose like a mushroom cloud, then slowly thinned out along the ceiling. Lena and Lisbeth had raved about the kitchen long before we moved, ever since they spent a week at Flat Willow, varnishing the long tables and benches in the dining hall. The tiles on the floor were small and reddish-orange. There must have been about a million pieces.

"Stay for coffee," Wipf Sanna-Pasel said as she gave the bell rope a few heaves. I had to make a quick decision. This was the morning I had planned to make myself scarce. It didn't matter if a boy missed lunch in the kuchel, but miss breakfast, dinner, or supper and the German schoolteacher was likely to ask questions. I decided to stay.

Like a clock ding-donging at the moment the big hand touches six or twelve, the people arrived. The women came from the slaughterhouse, and the men from the barns and workshops. The German teacher drove his tractor and trailer loaded with gardenboys and teenage girls. Hundreds of cucumbers covered the entire floor of the trailer. Soon the kitchen area was full of people. Everyone poured a cup of coffee at the trolley the cooks had wheeled to the middle of the floor, and took a shnecki biscuit or a wedge of sugarpie, then stood back against the walls. Coffee breaks were short. People didn't go into the dining hall during coffee breaks. Everybody crowded into the kitchen area and spilled into the corridors. Each person clasped hands together for a few seconds in a silent prayer before and after lunching. Some of the men were halfway out the door already as they folded their hands the second time.

A truck's brakes screeched outside. The cooks scurried

to finish packing the lunch chests for the men on the field. I slunk away to the corridor on the other side of the kitchen. I thought my father would leave right after he'd loaded the lunch chests, but he didn't. He came back in and walked across the kitchen area, his eyes searching the thinning croud.

"Is my Peter still here?" he asked.

Chickenman Jerg men pointed at me in the corridor.

"Peter, come with me to the combines this morning," my father said when he spotted me.

Heavens. Of all days — of all mornings to ask me along! Didn't he know I'd made important plans? Couldn't he have asked me later, in the afternoon?

I looked around me. Good. Uncle Josh wasn't there. "Josh-Vetter needs me at the goosebarn this morning," I said.

"Okay then," my father said. I watched him walk out the other side of the kuchel.

I knew he'd been looking forward to taking me to see the combines again. When he took children to see the combines, he always drove under the straw storm beside the combines with the truck windows rolled up. And he'd search our faces, smiling with delight. On the fields I sometimes had to look hard at my father because he didn't seem to be the same father who sat quietly at the table reading *The Western Producer* or *Reader's Digest*. On the fields he was like Olvetter. He talked about the good and the bad, the end of the world, and about sowing seeds. But somehow Judgement Day never seemed in front of you like a mirage on the field. It was to the sides, under you, and in the ditch among the green clover and grasses that the wind whipped about in whichever direction it wished. Afterwards he'd quiz us to see if we knew what he was talking about. When we'd give up, he wouldn't give us the answer, but tell us to keep thinking about it.

His favourite parable was about the harvest storm, which he'd tell after riding through it. "It's the one to take notice of," he'd say. "It comes after all the seeds have sprouted, the sun has pulled the grain out of the ground, the laws of God have cared for it and matured it, and then we can take it back and make it our own again. Until then, we can never be completely sure God will allow us to take it. Wherever there's seed, there's some kind of crop. It cannot be any other way. God does his work so thoroughly, so precisely and so constantly, that it's easy to forget He's even there. But He is. And He will allow every seed its time. In God's eyes, the weeds are no different from the wheat or barley crops. He loves them just as dearly. And he allows them to grow freely, although they may be a nuisance to people. And no matter how long a seed lays dormant in the granary or in the ground during the winter, or is stunted in a drought, sooner or later, it will repeat itself into the condition as the Law of God orders it."

I didn't understand what his parables about the wind and the seeds meant until later. But on that Saturday, on the first day the combines were out on Flat Willow soil, I wasn't even sure I cared. Maybe I *was* a lunatic. Maybe I was like Pierre. Maybe I couldn't think things through, either.

I tore out of the building as soon as my father's truck disappeared around the loop at the south end of the building. Why Sara was at the corner window of Olvetter's empty unit, I had no idea. I turned to look at the window as I raced by, and there she was, her head between the old curtains. She had no expression on her face. She quickly drew back when she saw me. I rushed on.

Chapter Sixteen

Tessa was sitting on the doorstep of the shack, waiting. She was wearing her blue jeans and white T-shirt and white sneakers. She stood up when she saw me, and smiled. I smiled back.

"You made it," she said.

"Yeah," I said.

"What's in the bag? A surprise?"

"A watermelon."

"A whole watermelon?"

"Yeah, a whole one."

She laughed. I think she knew, as I did, that our plan was crazy. We'd made it on Friday, when I'd run away again to the shack after slaughtering ducks. "Yuk," she had said. "You're covered with blood."

Her birthday was still one week away. But she was leaving that very afternoon with her cousin Holly, and she wasn't coming back. On her way back from British Columbia, her cousin was going to drop her off at her aunt's house in Calgary. Her father would come with the movers the week after.

"Well, here we are," she said.

"Yeah."

"What shall we do first?"

"I dunno."

Tessa turned. "Well, let's go into the shack," she said.

I followed her. It was cool inside. The shack pulled the air in one end and out the other. It was a perfect air-conditioner.

"See, I brought my ghetto blaster," she said.

"Wow." I put down the bag that held the watermelon and touched the music machine. It was all black with silver buttons, and one red one. The speakers had a grid in front.

Tessa looked at me curiously. "You're like Crocodile Dundee, coming to see the world for the first time," she said. "I can't imagine what it would be like without real music, or dancing."

I wanted to ask her who Crocodile Dundee was, but I didn't. She knew so much more than I did. I couldn't keep up with her. I said, "Oh, Lena and Lisbeth have a radio, and they've let me listen a few times. But they keep it hidden. If my father knew, he'd take it away."

She reached into a bag. "Ta da," she said.

"Dunce caps?"

"They're birthday hats, Peter."

I laughed. I'd never "celebrated" — like Tessa said — a birthday like this before. When I'd told Tessa that on my birthdays my mother always gave me a whole bottle of pop to drink, she had laughed and said we would at least do that.

She stretched out the elastic band of one birthday hat and placed it on her head. Then she stepped in front of me with the other one. "Take off your straw hat, you knucklehead," she said, and I laughed. I'd never thought I'd like it when someone called me a knucklehead.

She slipped the birthday hat on my head. I wished I had a mirror to see myself. I felt silly, but when I looked at Tessa, she was laughing, and the feeling went away.

"What's funny?"

"It's your hair. It sticks out like a lump of spaghetti."

I'd always had crazy hair. Hair that somehow managed to get kraupet all by itself. Even in church, when I had to comb it, I always had to starch it with a lot of soap to make it lay down.

I took the watermelon from the bag.

"What did your mom say about you taking a whole watermelon?" Tessa asked.

"She doesn't know."

"You stole it?"

"Yeah," I said, and Tessa shook her head. I had stolen it while the adults were at breakfast in the kuchel and hidden it in the goosebarn.

"How do you intend to eat it, Peter?"

"Well, I thought maybe we can just lay it on a board and cut off slices with my pocket knife."

I didn't tell her it was the same knife that I'd used to cut gopher tails off the gophers and scrape cow manure off my shoes.

"Okay," she said. "You're the watermelon boss."

When I cut it, I had to cut all around the watermelon, because my knife was so short. Lord, that cut was lopsided. It had a funny shape in the middle that stood up like a shale boulder in a middle of a field. But at least I had it open. I cut off a huge slice, and it was even more lopsided: two inches thick on one end with almost nothing on the other. Tessa watched me slice the watermelon and I thought she was going to have a heart attack, laughing.

"Sorry, Peter," she said. "You are so funny. You should be a comedian."

I handed her the piece of watermelon, then cut one for myself.

As soon as we sat down, Tessa said, "Oh, I forgot the music." She stood up and pushed the button of the music machine. It was the kind of music I'd heard in the mall in Lethbridge, a kind of floaty music. Tessa knew about music. She'd told me about different kinds. There was country music and rock-and-roll, and something called classic. She sure knew a lot about classic.

"See, that's classical music," she said. She sat down beside me on the plank. We ate watermelon and listened to the music float all over the shack. The music made me feel strange, as if I was sitting there in just my pyjamas.

"I'll miss you, Peter," she said.

I didn't say anything, but I knew I'd miss her too. When I thought about her, I still got goosebumps because of her spookiness, but somehow I knew that wherever she went, she'd be in God's corner. She wasn't in the ark, but I thought she was at least on dry land. I was glad my father had told me about letting God decide about people's souls. And when I looked at her rosy face, and at her big blue eyes, it was still hard to believe that I had kissed her. Actually, *she* had kissed *me*, but being real cool, as Tessa had said I was, I figured that made me practically irresistible. It was just a mishap that Hufer Maria back at Rockyview hadn't ever grabbed hold of me and given me a kiss. But Ronni Kleinser and the other boys, boy, those suckle-kids were stupid, running after gophers for jawbreakers. Those guys had a lot to learn.

I remembered what Tessa had told me the evening before, about her plans. Someday she would go to university and study to be a journalist.

"What will you write about?" I had asked her.

"About you. And I'll come back and interview you on TV."

"Really?"

"No, I'm just kidding."

"Well, you could," I said. "I wouldn't mind."

She thought about it for a minute. "Well, maybe I'll write fiction books in my spare time, books like *The Catcher in the Rye* and *Of Mice and Men*, or about a certain crazy cowboy who spies on two girls swimming in a dugout and gets stung by wasps and has to jump into the dugout to save his life."

I laughed. "That would be me."

"That's very observant of you," she said.

Then she looked at me seriously and said, "What if I made up a story about a certain girl named Luba, in Russia or some place like that? And what if her dad were sick for many years, till he had nothing left because of his illness? His children would starve, and his wife would run away with a rich man. Everybody would hate Luba's father and disbelieve everything he says because he would have told so many lies to everybody already. The only one who'd still believe him is Luba, because she just wouldn't be able to stop loving him."

"Wow. That would be some story," I said.

"But there would also be a man named Vladimir and an evil ogre in the story who hate each other. See, the evil ogre would have all these guns that he gives to the people in the village."

"Wow."

"One day Vladimir would get really mad at the evil ogre and set out to kill the ogre and all his friends. But then Luba, who'll hate the evil ogre too, would steal a dagger out of the ogre's truck while he's drinking vodka in the pork factory."

"Why a dagger, Tessa?" I said. "There has to be a reason." I knew a few things about mysteries from all the stuff Sara told me.

Tessa had given me an impatient look. "There are always daggers in mystery stories, you knucklehead," she had said.

Now, Tessa nudged me. "Peter, you're day-dreaming again. It's my birthday party, remember?"

"Oh," I said, sitting up straight.

Tessa stood up and carved off another lopsided wedge of watermelon. She handed it to me and cut a piece for herself.

"We'll never eat all that," she said. "The flies are coming for it. Why didn't you bring just a few slices?"

"I had to hide it in the goosebarn for a few hours. It would've got all mushy."

Tessa shook her head. "You needn't have bothered."

"But I wanted to bring it, Tessa. I wanted to give you something for your birthday."

We were silent for a minute. Outside, far away, I could

hear the combines. A truck honked. It was probably a truck driving under the combine auger, getting ready to take a load of grain.

Tessa sat down beside me. "Peter," she said.

"What?"

"Close your eyes."

"Why?" I asked, although I knew what was coming.

"Just close them, you'll see," she said.

I closed my eyes, but I had a hard time keeping still. I heard the boards move. And then I got a cool watermelony kiss.

Sara had told me it was best to keep your eyes closed when you kiss. Unless it was in the dark. But I opened my eyes just for a peek. Tessa's eyes were open too. We exploded with laughter.

Tessa stopped laughing and gave me a serious look. "Peter, thank you for coming back, and for being my friend." And she held my hand. I liked it when she held my hand and squeezed it. I just smiled and squeezed back. Her hand was warm and soft.

"Am I the first girl who kissed you?" she said.

"Yeah — well, Sara kissed me once, but that doesn't count. She's my sister. She just needed to practise."

"Practise?"

"Yeah. When people get fourteen years old, they start going together with the boys and girls in the "crowd" when guests come. And they play spin-the-bottle and hang-on-the-doorknob."

"Hang-on-the-doorknob?"

"It's some sort of kissing game. Sara used to tell me about that stuff."

"I wish I had met Sara," Tessa said. "You talk about her a lot."

"But she's not the same any more. She's always suspicious of everybody. She's afraid I'll turn into a drinker like my brother."

Tessa shook her head. "You'll never be a drinker."

"How do you know?"

"You won't."

"I might be one. Jake was never a drinker, even when he was fifteen he wasn't. But then he worked one winter in the pigbarn with the pigman and he started drinking. And now he uses up all his pelt money to buy booze."

Tessa stood up and put her hands on her hips. "Peter Waldner, you will not be a drinker," she said. "I just know you won't be one." Then she put her hands on my shoulders and shook me a little. "I hereby pronounce you not a drinker, forever and ever. Okay?"

I laughed. I sure hoped she was right.

The music had stopped. Tessa pulled a tape from the bag. "Let's play a different kind of music now," she said.

She changed the tapes and turned the knob. When the music started, it was louder. I liked it much better. It was Lisbeth's kind.

Tessa picked up the bottle of pop she had brought with her and twisted the cap off. She took a long swig; her throat worked fervently. When she came up for air, she let out a satisfied breath and a burp. And she laughed like a maniac. I liked it when she acted crazy. She handed me the bottle, and I took a long swallow.

"Drink it all," she said.

As I guzzled it down I remembered The Cowboy Kid. When the bottle was empty I burped too, and yelled "Yahoo" as loud as I could.

"Shall we dance then, cowboy?" Tessa asked in her sing-song voice, and I knew she was flirting again. I had no idea how to dance, but I figured I'd just imitate Lisbeth and swing my shoulders and tap my feet a little.

"Here now, place your right arm on my shoulder," she said. "Let's do the two-step." She took my left hand in her right hand. I started tapping my feet like Lisbeth and swinging my shoulders with the music. Boy, I liked that music. It had a jumpy sound, and you couldn't help wanting to bounce along with it. BOOM BA BA, BOOM BA BA, BOOM BA BA. Tessa gave up trying to show me how to move, she was laughing so hard at how I shuffled my feet and tapped them at the same time. I just went crazy with the music. Maybe it was all that watermelon, and that pop fizzing in my stomach, but at that moment I didn't care about cows and about being extremely religious, or the Chronicles. I didn't even think about people back at Flat Willow working in the heat, while I danced like a lunatic in the shade of an old shack out in the world. Boy, I loved that fiddle in there, and that wailing sound. The guitars twanged and howled like a son-of-a-gun.

Tessa danced right along with me. Before I knew it, she was trying to imitate me. I figured it was because I was so good at dancing. I was good at a lot of things, and dancing, I guessed, was one of them. BOOM BA BA, BOOM BA BA. She swung her shoulders, her hips, arms, everything. Then she sort of crouched down and shook her whole body like a cat shakes water off her fur. She was plain crazy, that English girl. And throughout all the dancing, she kept laughing — if I didn't know better, I'd have said she'd guzzled down a little booze.

She stopped long enough to say, "Peter, you know how you dance?"

"How?"

"You dance like Pierre used to dance."

I shrugged. "Oh well." I didn't care how I danced. I figured there was only one way to do it. Just swing your shoulders and tap your feet. No need to follow one step, two step, BOOM BA BA, BOOM BA BA. Those rules weren't for me.

"Really, you do," Tessa said. "That's how Pierre always danced at the barn dances. He danced with everybody, little kids and teenagers and old ladies."

I was sweating now, and Tessa's forehead was shiny too.

She sang along to a song called "Ghost Riders in the Sky." Halfway through the song, she picked a small board off the floor. She pretended it was a fiddle, and made fancy, bouncy steps with her feet. She was a good dancer too. The floor of the shack creaked and moaned, and the loose boards leaped up and down to her dancing.

"Dance, Peter," she called out when I stopped to wipe sweat off my face with my shirt hanging from my pants. It was the craziest and spookiest thing I'd ever heard of, to dance like a retarded man. But I figured, what the hell, I was probably a lunatic just like Pierre had been, so why not dance like him too?

"Should I dance like a poor man?" I laughed.

"Yeah, dance like a poor man, you knucklehead."

Then there was an even bouncier song called "La Bamba". By the time that one was finished, my shirt clung to my skin as if I'd taken a dive into a dugout. Lord, it was hot in the shack now.

When the music stopped, Tessa plopped herself on the plank and just sat there, panting. She wiped the sweat off her forehead with her T-shirt.

Suddenly a shadow moved. It was the strangest thing. It was like the sun going behind a cloud, although there were no clouds that day. The shadow moved across the wall. I had the feeling someone was looking at us. It happened very fast. Two faces moved into the busted-out window. They weren't smiling. They belonged to my father and Sara.

Chapter Seventeen

A dust devil whirled and whipped the grass outside the shack, then moved along the coulee. My father stepped into the doorway. He was big; his eyes seemed hard. My arms were flung against the wall of the shack. I trembled and looked at Tessa. Her face had no expression. Sara stood behind my father, and when he stepped into the shack, she pushed past him. She stared at Tessa, then scurried to the empty pop bottle and lifted it to her nose.

"Father, it's just orange," she said.

"It was the watermelon he was carrying," my father said, pointing to the lopsided watermelon on the plank.

He looked at Tessa, then at me. "Sit down," he said.

Tessa edged close to her music machine, and put her hand on it. Sara was eyeing the tapes.

"Are you Stan Longman's girl?" my father said.

"Yes, I am, sir," Tessa said. She gave my father a little smile, but he didn't smile back.

"Is your father home today?"

"No sir, my cousin Holly is."

"Does she know you're here?"

"Yes, sir."

"You don't have to call me sir," my father said. "I'm not a soldier."

He looked at me, then back to Tessa. "Has Peter been over at your farm?"

Tessa looked at me quickly, then froze her stare on the ground. She said nothing. My father nodded knowingly.

"Besides the music, did you do anything sinful?"

Tessa seemed puzzled. "What do you mean?" she said.

My father shook his head. "Oh, never mind." He was quiet for a moment. He sat down on the plank a few feet from me. Sara sat beside him.

"So what does your father do when you do something you shouldn't?" my father asked.

Tessa shrugged. "Nothing."

"He never gives you a strapping?"

"No."

"Tell me, have you ever done something to deserve a strapping?"

Tessa nodded.

"And your father didn't strap you?"

"No."

My father took off his straw hat and ran his hand through his hair. "What have you told Peter?" he asked. "Have you tried to convert him to your religion?"

Tessa gave my father a bold stare. "Why would I do that, Mr. Waldner? The last thing Peter needs is a different religion. He doesn't even understand his own yet."

My father smiled then. "You're a very bright girl," he said. "Do you understand your own religion?"

"A little."

Sara tugged at Father's arm. "Father, ask her about the gun — "

"Sara, be quiet now. Let me talk."

He turned back to Tessa. "Do you believe in the pope?"

Tessa lifted her eyebrows and stared at my father. She seemed to be thinking hard. "I believe in God," she said.

"What about Jesus? Do you believe in Jesus Christ?"

Tessa frowned. "Do you?"

"I asked you."

Tessa said another bold thing. "Why do you people argue so much about religion?"

My father laughed. "Why? Did my boy argue with you?"

"He thinks about hell a lot," she said, giving me a weak smile.

My father laughed again. "So there is hope for my boy yet. An apple doesn't fall far from the tree."

"But why do you need to argue?"

"I wouldn't call it arguing," he said firmly. "A believer whose light shines only from lamps fitting the climate of the day, and who doesn't bear fruit with an exemplary lifestyle, is a pseudo-believer, a coward. It is proper for my boy to express his beliefs to the world."

Sara was nodding to every word Father was saying, but her eyes were on Tessa, whose eyes moved back and forth between the three of us on the plank. I wondered if Tessa understood my father's words. I sure didn't.

My father turned to me then. "Peter, did she — look up now, look on my face — did she tell you who threw that gun in the slough?"

"Yes."

"Who?"

"Kleinser Sommel and his brother Joel."

Tessa scratched nervously at her music machine.

"Girl, why don't you tell my boy what really happened?" my father said.

There was a long silence. Tessa bit her lip; she seemed terribly nervous. When she spoke, her voice wavered. "I'm sorry, Peter, I was afraid you'd be mad at us for blaming your people, and — "

"Just tell him, girl."

"I tried to tell him, sir, but he didn't catch on."

"Tell him what he didn't catch on to."

Tessa stood up and walked toward me. She reached out to touch my hand, but I jerked it away. My father was too near.

"I was the one who stole Mr. Clements' gun," Tessa said. "They were all in the pigbarns that Saturday night. Mr. Clements, my dad and...the fat pigman and his two brothers. Aunt Mae had fallen asleep on the couch, so I ran across the coulee in the moonlight. I was worried about my dad. When he drank Mr. Clements' moonshine he always got so drunk he could hardly walk."

My father cleared his throat. "So tell him how you stole the gun."

Tessa frowned, and continued. "As I walked from behind the barns, I saw the two younger brothers returning Mr. Clements' gun to his truck. They'd been shooting targets."

"And?" my father said.

"I waited till they were in the barn till I took the gun and carried it down to the slough. You have to understand. If Pierre had gotten hold of that gun...."

"So you took the law into your own hands?"

Tessa leaned against the wall and said, "I guess so."

"But why not let the police, or a doctor, deal with a situation like that? Didn't your father or uncle know that a man inclined to go after someone with a gun ought to be put in a place where he would be restrained?"

"They'd already warned us twice that they'd take Pierre away from us. Just like they took Pierre away from Uncle Frank's brother Earl many years ago, when he was sixteen. Pierre murdered his grandfather, you know."

My scalp crawled.

"And you housed a murderer?" my father said.

"He was taking treatments. It was either live with us, or live in some hole in the city. If those men hadn't shot the rabbits, or if Pierre hadn't seen them shoot the pigs and slit their throats — "

"The man was dangerous," my father said, "but the point is, you and your father tried to put the blame on our people. Does your father realize how much trouble we go to in order to stay on the good side of the law? There are neighbours around here who still believe that our boys might have been responsible for your poor man's death."

Tessa took a step toward my father. "How did you know all this, anyway, Mr. Waldner?" she asked. "Did my dad tell you?"

My father grinned. "I know the neighbours. They tell me things. Now, I didn't know the real truth till you told me just now, but between what I heard from the neighbours" — he glanced at me — "and what my other son told me, I had a pretty good notion." He put his arm around Sara. "Where do you think this girl gets her detective nose from?"

Sara beamed proudly. "Father, ask her if she knows why the poor man walked out into a blizzard."

"Nobody knows," he said. "Unless there is something the Longmans aren't telling us." He turned to Tessa. "Is there something you aren't telling us?"

Tessa shook her head sadly. "No."

"Well, He often comes like a thief in the night," my father said. "And, although there is always a reason, we can't know them all."

He turned to me then. "And you, do you realize what you have done?"

I didn't answer.

"Answer me. Do you realize what you have done?"

"Yes."

"So what should happen now?"

I shrugged.

My father shook his head. "Do you not listen at church? Where is your head? Do you not listen to your grandfather, to your mother and me? Do you not listen to your German teacher when he tells you about what you can and can't do?"

I stared at the floor, and stayed quiet.

My father took hold of my arm then, and stood up, pulling me with him. "Get out of this shack," he said firmly.

As I tripped out of the shack, he turned to Tessa. "You go home too," he said. "Find someone from your own people to carry on with."

We walked down the coulee, my father, Sara and I. Up ahead, on the other side of the shelterbelt, the bell rang. I glanced back to the shack quickly. Tessa was waiting for me to turn. She waved. But I didn't wave back.

When we were deep in the coulee, and the shack had disappeared from view, my father told Sara to run ahead. Sara touched my hand. "Please don't be angry at me, Peter. I was worried about you."

I couldn't be angry at Sara.

My father gave her a push. "Sara. I told you. Go now."

She ran off, but turned often to look back. My father pulled his pocket knife from his pocket and stooped down to cut off a willow sapling.

"Bend over," he said.

He gripped the top of my pants and stretched them tight. The blows on my rear were hard, and the pain shot down my legs in electric shocks. The shelterbelt at the coulee edge swam in my vision, as if I was out in the flood, reaching for the ark. I counted the strokes, but lost count after six. My father talked in a low and carefully articulated voice between blows. "You should know better. You have to learn the rules. You may not realize it now, but I mean you good. You are my responsibility. It is my obligation to the community and to God Almighty to discipline you."

Afterwards, he threw the sapling to the grass, and picked up his straw hat where it had fallen. He walked away and started up the coulee. I sat on the grass, sobbing quietly. Memories from the last two weeks floated like ice-patches on water. I was afloat on a lone patch. A part of me wanted to shake my fist at the ark and curse at everything in it, yet another part wanted to hang on, to belong, to reach out to my father, to run after him and be with him.

Someone touched my shoulder. I jerked my head up. Tessa stood beside me. She knelt down in front of me in the grass.

"I'm sorry, Peter," she said, putting her sweaty arms around me and squeezing me. I rested my head on her shoulder and wiped my tears on her T-shirt. Then she placed my straw hat back on my head, and fussed a little with the collar of my checkered shirt.

"Your collar is all crooked, you crazy cowboy," she said.

I looked up to Flat Willow. My father had stopped at the side of the coulee.

"Go away, Tessa," I said, pushing her from me, "before my father comes back."

"Like hell I will," she said.

"You'd better. See, he's coming back."

"I'm not leaving."

"Please, Tessa. He'll whip you too."

"He won't," she said firmly. "He's not stupid."

She threw her arms around me and held me, as if to hold me down lest a tornado sweep me up and hurl me away into a black cloud.

I saw my father's black legs appear, and I heard his black workshoes swish in the grass. The closer he came, the tighter Tessa hugged me. His feet stopped. Nobody spoke. I looked up. My father was looking back to Flat Willow. His truck was parked at the end of the shelterbelt, on the other side. Sara stood at the barbed-wire fence, waiting. My father moved to the side, blocking the sun. Still, he didn't speak.

He crouched down and I looked up for a moment. The sun hit my face, and I had to squeeze my eyes shut until the glare of its ghost had melted away inside my head. When I let the light in again, my father's suntanned face was in front of me.

He tapped Tessa's shoulder. "Have you ever gone through a combine storm, girl?"

My English friend shook her head. "No, sir, I haven't."

My father extended his hand. "Would you like to?"

Tessa hesitated. "Please don't beat Peter any more, Mr. Waldner," she said.

"He's had his punishment, girl," he said.

"Promise?"

My father laughed. He glanced back to where Sara was standing at the fence, and shook his head. I knew what he was thinking.

"Let's go," he said, and Tessa slowly let go of me and took my father's hand.

The three of us walked up the coulee. My father walked ahead of Tessa and me. Nobody spoke. Tessa was shaking, and she stared at the ground. When she looked up, she smiled weakly. I felt strange. I wondered what my father would say in the truck. I hoped he would quiz Tessa about the meaning of his parables. Especially about the seeds. I wondered if she would catch on. One thing I knew was when my father threw the willow sapling to the grass, he had let go both ends of the stick. In my mind — because I was an artist, I could see clearly — I saw *my* wicked old sticks. I gave them a mighty fling. The wind my father had talked about, the wind that blew where it wished, picked them up and whisked them away into space. I think some of those damned old sticks landed back at the old colony, or maybe even further back, in the Old Country.

Then I realized I was carrying a brand new stick. It was strong enough to stretch across the coulee and walk across on. Tessa held the other end. I knew that someday I would cross that coulee again.

About the author

Samuel Hofer was born in a Hutterite community in Alberta. In 1968, when he was six years old, the community branched out, and he moved to southern Saskatchewan. In the Hutterite colony he was a gardenboy, stockboy, rockpicker, feedmill operator, manurespreader operator, backhoe operator, construction worker, painter and much more. In his teens he spent much of his free time drawing cartoons, selling many to *The Western Producer* under the pseudonym of Sommel, his Tyrolese name. Because of increasing frustrations with having to keep his cartooning ideas hidden, and because of an interest in eastern religions and philosophies, he left the Hutterite lifestyle in 1983. His plan was to become a freelance cartoonist. But, realizing people's interest in the Hutterite culture, he began selling traditional Hutterite recipes by mail order instead while working on a chicken farm near Melville, Saskatchewan. That led to moving off the farm to live in Saskatoon. In 1986 he published the best-selling *Hutterite Treasury of Recipes. How to Turn Your Artwork and Cartoons into Cash* came a year later. It was a financial flop. But in 1988, while living in Red Deer, Alberta, *Soups and Borschts* got him back into the book business. In 1991, he published *Born Hutterite*, a book of short stories. *The Hutterite Community Cookbook* was published a year later. *Dance like a Poor Man* is his first novel. He now lives and writes in Winnipeg.

Dance like a Poor Man

Also by Samuel Hofer

Cookbooks

* *The Hutterite Treasury of Recipes*
Soups and Borschts
True and Basic Ethnic Cooking
The Hutterite Community Cookbook

Art and Business

* *How to Turn Your Artwork and Cartoons into Cash*

Fiction

Born Hutterite

* Out of print